From Carmen Maronii the Journalist;

My name is Carmen Maronii and I am a journalist. I have done stories from Girls missing, to normal everyday columns in the school paper. I would say I am a hidden to the core skeptic and realist. I may be a junior journalist, but my creativity and eye for the strange, different and ear for the information and talk gives me the edge to get the story out and take the strange cases. This is of course my 3rd year in, but I don't see why I can't be a pro now. I know some of my peers find me a little irritating and loose cannon, but that never stopped the stories and the leads from coming to knock at my dorm room at midnight or later. I do what others find so hard to, I give everything I got to get the job and story the life it is screaming for.

I choose the strange, the weird and the most difficult of cases, because it is a test it is journalism the world will not stop being what it is just because something to another is different and strange. I see that my case of extreme has yet to take shape and form, but I believe this case and story will set the record and the strange a new scale. They don't call me Maronii the Journalist for nothing. I work and write for the AAP it is fun, lively and our creative senior journalist knows what strange and stories are all about. Megan Parex the senior journalist some say I am to take over once she graduates I am looking forward to that, but let's first see what has happened to Stacy Dugal?

The Journalist series will give you the in now and the out later. Being a journalist has a lot of responsibilities and its problems too. I love it, the good the bad and the confusing. All of the hidden information and more, It is what gave me the story I give to you today take a read and come on this journey with me.

-Carmen Maronii; Journalist

Disappearance of Stacy Dugal: Chapter 1

Hello, my readers this is Carmen Maronii your junior Journalist for your paper that brings you, Current, Correct and Full of Flavor News. Welcome to AAP for Hawkins School for Girls. This month's Column will focus on all details surrounding the Disappearance of Freshman Student Stacy Dugal. The administrators would like to reiterate that if anyone, knows any information on this puzzling situation, please do quickly as possible contact your Schools Administrative team.

The date was March 3rd 2010, exactly three days before the masquerade ball; they've been having this since 1910, basically since the school was founded.

One night late in my dorm room I received a phone call from one of my co-journalists Amy Stevenson telling me of how there were cops everywhere on Midas Rowe at the Freshman Dorm. I immediately put on my clothes and rushed over. When I got to the dorm it was at least 20 cops and an ambulance and a fire truck and kids everywhere. So doing some investigating around the dorm with the students I found out that a freshman named Stacey Liza Dugal, 18 was not in her dorm room. Me thinking to myself well that's still no reason to be having an emergency system concert out here at 11:00 at night on a School night. It had to be more to it. My stomach was telling me that. So I had to follow it...

Stacy Dugal's Roomy Celine Norman: Chapter 2

I walked around with my Favorite Reporter pad and pen, and my reading glasses, looking for anyone standing out as seeming to know more about this puzzling situation than they led on. I came across one Celine Norman a roomy with the alleged disappeared. I approached her not seeming so eager to know if Stacy Dugal was dead or if this was a hoax or if the girl just simply went home, or with a boyfriend. She seemed to be real shaken up and was crying terribly.

"Hi, Celine I'm Maroni-she cut me off before I could even finish my name and said so obviously..." "I know who you are. Turning around so tense and mean looking her tears dried up quickly and she smoothed her hair back and smirked at me....Your Carmen Maronii the infamous journalist on campus."

I looked at her surprisingly, now normally I would be flattered because let's just face it I have put in work and I love what I do, but this girl; this Celine she seemed utterly anxious to meet me.
"Okay so you know who I am, now can you tell me what's going on here or are you going to play a hard source for me? She smiled and said can you walk with me? With no hesitation I said yes and

began to listen."

Celine Norman: "Well around 10:45pm I came in from a late night over from Hawkins Brother School. I came into the dorm spoke to an um; Lisa Fredrick's had a laugh or two with her and then headed up the stairs. I then heard a thump I didn't pay any attention to it because honestly Maronii, girls are going to do what they want regardless of restriction or consequences and the more prone is the newbie's."

She looked over to me to and smirked while she told me this, we continued to walk and talk, by now we've passed the sophomore dorm and started to see the ambulance and fire truck leaving<

"So as I got closer to our dorm room I pulled out my key and that's when I heard another loud thump and this time it was right in front of me, meaning in our room. I hurried and unlocked the door and pushed the door open, when I did there was nothing, not even Stacy. Her bed was unmade her shoes still there it was like she was there, but wasn't, I look around the room and that's when I saw it-..."

Out of nowhere like a truck in your living room a campus security guard interrupted our walk and told us to get back to our dorms curfew is still in effect. I turned around to tell Celine that I would catch up with her later but she was gone. I began heading back to my room when something caught my eye, Celine running into the Forbidden Tree's and opposite direction of her dorm. I got out my phone to take a Quick snap, and then ran back to my room.

Walking into my room I sit my pad down and my phone open up my laptop and began to upload the picture I took of Celine running into the Forest. I began looking through my notes as I was waiting on the picture to upload to my laptop. I went back through the part of Celine's story where she said "Girls are going to do what they want regardless of restriction, consequences". By now the picture was uploaded. I began hovering over it with the mouse trying to see if there was anything I didn't see in the dark. Hovering over the picture I could see where Celine was reaching for something within her back pocket that I hadn't seen while interviewing her. I began to take notes on this picture and its contents that had only just appeared to me, while doing that I received a knock on my door, by now it was 12:25 midnight who could be at my door this late.

Counselor Ms. Jameson: Chapter 3

Opening up the door, to my surprise it was Counselor Beverly Jameson, the freshman student's head counselor.

"Hello, Miss Jameson what are you doing here at 12 AT NIGHT?"

“Sorry to stop by I know you were probably busy…”

I let her in and immediately ran over to my laptop slammed it shut and closed my pad. <

“Well you know; I am just up looking over tomorrow’s column for the AAP. What can I do for you Ms. Jameson?”

“I was wondering if you had heard about all the commotion tonight over on Midas.”

“Well yes, I received a phone call indicating there might be a story there? Why?”

“Yes, a story… What I’m about to tell you has to be kept off the record, unless some news comes back otherwise. UNDERSTOOD Maronii??”

“Of course, do you mind if I do take notes?”

“Yes of course, but I want you to know if any of what I am about to tell you comes out I will deny it and I will pursue the termination of your seat on the AAP?”

“Totally understood, have a seat why don’t you…”

She looked a nervous wreck; she had on sweat pants and a pink Hawkins Girls school shirt on with our logo and mascot “Fierce, Females make their own Way” and our mascot of the Cat that represents our school”, with blue bedroom shoes and a bonnet on her head. It’s like she was woken up to the news like I was, but something had her seriously devastated. I was itching to know what that was.

“You can go ahead Ms. Jameson I am listening.”

Ms. Jameson: “Okay, two days ago Stacy Dugal came to my office, late one night much disoriented and very, upset. I assumed she was just upset because everyone knew that she was caught over at Hawkins School for Boys? It did not hit me that she might have been upset about something else. So I invite her in and gave her some tea, and a tissue. She began rambling on about the girl’s freshman dorm and this rumor going on that she was a lesbian. I immediately asked her what she meant. She just said, “There out to get me I just know it.” I asked her who? And she just looked at me gave me the tissue back and walked out. Ever since that night I have been wondering what she was talking about, but I guess tonight is a part of that.”

So Ms. Jameson you had no idea who might be causing Stacy so much grief in her dorm?

She just looked at me like she had more to say, and at the same time she couldn't believe I had the nerve to insinuate that she might know more; but any information I was going to further get out of her I killed that little fly. No sooner than I said that she hopped up

Said "that's all, I've said enough already. I must go, goodnight Maronii."

I had no time to respond I just let her go. But one thing I did know she knew what was going on and so did Celine and all the girls in that dorm, I just had to find out what they were hiding.

I went back to look at the photo and my notes, going through them again I also noticed something a little odd...Ms. Jameson had said and I quote "I assumed she was upset because everyone knew that she was caught over at Hawkins School for Boys" hmmm? What did she mean she was caught and if so, what did Ms. Jameson mean everyone knew? It's the first time I am hearing about it.

Now this is what you my readers need to understand, Ms. Jameson is the Freshman counselor, if you attend Hawkins at all Boys or Girls you know that all dorms are divided between Freshman to senior dorms and every dorm has its own counselor, Head of Household, but the school has One dean and that is Dean Lily for Hawkins Girls and Dean Greggs over at Hawkins Boys. Now if Stacy was afraid of something in her dorm the only people that would know are the ones within that dorm.

Secrets don't just surface into other dorms unless it is so severe someone has accidentally slipped upon it, because no freshman are to enter junior, sophomore or senior dorms and vice versa. The classes are in one building, but still if something has happened within the dorm it still could be kept private because the dorm has its own rules separate from the whole schools. I just shake my head for a while and underline Ms. Jameson's quote as well as Celine's. I must get to bed I have class at 11 this morning. I do know 3 thing's for sure, Ms. Jameson knew more and Celine knew more and I was going to find out continuing after class.<

Class is in Session: Chapter 4

It's 11 am and I am heading to class I look over my notes again. I couldn't help but to keep thinking about my underlined quotes both from Ms. Jameson and Celine. I had to get into that dorm, but how. After classes kids are allowed to roam, but not like that. Hmm... coming to a halt I run into Jacob Peninsky, he works for the year, book club and standing there looking at him I couldn't help, but to think if something more was to this. I knew there had to be something in the pictures he had taken within the last week from all the school functions leading up until the Masquerade Ball. This is the annual Ball so I know there were a lot of pictures taken so far and a lot more the night of the ball. I go over to Jacob...

Introducing Jacob Peninsky...

"Hey! Have you taken any pictures of any of the functions?"

"What's up Maronii, you only talk to me when you need to use the cherry room, or you need to how I can put this...ugh use me."

I giggle, and then quickly step back into my investigative tactics.

Now some are probably thinking if you're new to my columns, and stories and articles all that jazz. Why is there a boy in the girl's school? Well special arrangements were made for Peninsky; let's just say he has a little more sugar than Betty Crocker's cake. There were several boys at Hawkins Girls School, but these boys were either a little challenged or special in other ways like Peninsky here. All together there were 10 boys, at Hawkins Girls, and these guys had their own dorm, sort of like everyone else's dorm, but just them. They fit right in and they stayed out of trouble to. Well that's the M11 on that subject.

"So are you saying that you do have those pictures, Peninsky?"

"I am saying Maronii, if you are looking to cook up something about what happened last night over on Midas, you need to drop it. Digging in a back yard that is unfamiliar to you, is good to no one. So drop it will you?"

Whoa, did he really just say that. Ha, ha, ha that is what I needed to confirm that this was going to be my biggest story yet.

"What? I am just taking a little bit of notes. Nothing is wrong with that."

I giggle and continue to take my notes.

"No you're not you damn, detective. Why are you doing this to me Maronii? I have given you photos before and we almost always got caught. I feel like we are always doing something dirty. Yuck, girls! OMG!!! I am going to need a shot of water."

"Oh, stop it you big drama queen, we will do what we always do. You go to your work station like always over in Hawkins Activities Lab and of course I'll be over there in the Journalist department, and we'll just put in late hours. Okay!"

"Yes, yes I hear you. Don't we need a late work pass for that. It's not going to work I am telling you it's not going to work."

He was starting to make a scene and the other students were looking at us, I had to get this Queen under control, before everyone knew what we were up to, before we actually knew what we were up to.

"Calm, down Peninsky, its Thursday we do not need any permission on Thursdays."

"Yes, okay I'm calming down."

"So just do what you normally do and make sure you have out all the pictures from this past week and this one leading up until today."

"Okay, I will just make sure that you are down in the lab after the last class, which is at 8pm."

"I most certainly will, see you later."

We do our little friend handshake and go into different directions.] [I continue to head to class which starts in 5 minutes, and Ms. Lexington is not going to be happy if I walk in their 1 minute before she locks the door. In her eyes it's disrespectful.

Running to her class I make it there exactly 2 minutes before 12 noon, I yay myself and get into the class. Soon as I walk in she stops from taking the roll, and says...

"CARMEN LARIZZA MARONII!"

"Yes Ms. Lexington?"

"So I see you grace us with your lateness once again this week?"

"Not technically Ms. Lexington, your rule is and I quote..." If one shall be late to Advance Journalism by 1 minute before instruction, they will be locked out and immediately written up as absent".

Everyone stopped and looked at me then looked at her, she sat her roster down and looked at me then walked over. I was so scared

"SIT DOWN, Maronii before I put you out, UNDERSTOOD? Now quote that."

She turns around and walks back to her desk. Stopping dead in the middle of the row, she turns around and looks to me and say's...

"Nice Listening."

Then winks at me!

"See this is what journalism is all about students, listening, observing and being precise. Let's take Carmen for example she was not "TECHNICALLY late", but I still saw her as late. She immediately took from my own rules and regulations and gave me my own lesson in listening and being observant. Now who knows why this is important out there in the real world of facts, lies, hidden truths, big hurdles and barriers to get to the truth, justice and... as well as Why it is not so much as important in here when it applies to my rules...Who can finish this for me?"

She looks around and I raise my hand, but she goes to Rebecca Chasten

"Yes Ms. Chasten... what do you have to add to this?"

Rebecca Chasten: "In adding Ms. Lexington..."

She looks at me smiles and rolls her eyes.

Now Rebecca and I have been frienemies for some time now, starting at the competition for the junior journalist for AAP, we ran head to head and it was a vicious campaign, but Rebecca did the dumbest and most desperate thing a person could do once they feel like they are losing at something they want and there not use to losing....

She made up a story about the Senior Journalist Megan Parex. Megan is an awesome girl, but her problem was that she was friends with Rebecca and Rebecca didn't think she should have to run, that she should just be handed the seat. Megan was not going to do that, so Rebecca went after her in her campaign. Stating that Megan was falsifying information within the AAP about articles that she had written that was her own work, the problem with this lie was there was no type of facts and stable evidence to back up Rebecca's claim and she sort of picked on the wrong Journalist, let's just be blunt here Megan did not become Senior Journalist of one of the Top schools in the country, by slacking on her work.

She pursued being a journalist like I since high school and she continued that study all through college up until her Sophomore year when she did the piece on Hawkins Masquerade Ball Mystery of 1950, that won her the respect and the seat Senior Journalist of the AAP and she has held it since, I was a freshman when she was a sophomore and now she is a senior and I am a junior. Someone has to take her place when the year ends and she goes off to Graduate or whatever she chooses to do and let's just say I have my eye on that beautiful seat.

So Rebecca, lied and Megan being a journalist went to her first rule in journalism..."Never write about something or someone that facts will not write themselves" She taught me the rules and the tricks, so I knew she wasn't going down like that when this rumor surfaced. Rebecca continued to accuse Megan one day at a School pep rally for the Girls Volleyball team that were heading into championships down in Texas. She came down onto the gym floor and took the stand from Megan and continued her lies and scandal.

Megan let Rebecca finish her radical truth and then told a volleyball player I forgot that girl's name, to turn off the lights and turn on the projector. The girl did just that, then up came all of Megan's notes and briefs and copies and pictures and website listings and teacher notes and finally her completed article on the Hawkins Masquerade Ball Mystery of 1950. She ended that with, this statement to Rebecca and all the students and I quote "Never write about something or someone that facts will not write themselves." After that all the students clapped and booed Rebecca off the court. Ever since then Rebecca has been trying her hardest to get me and Megan, because after her little episode the students voted me Junior Journalist, and she was looked as a manipulator and a liar.]

Rebecca: "In adding Ms. Lexington, It is important---"

Ms. Lexington cuts Rebecca off, Rebecca just had this look of pure shock and I couldn't help but to laugh.

"I don't want you to answer that I want Carmen to answer that, but what I do want you to answer is my ending statement the last word of that...Can you?"

She sighs and then says...

Rebecca: "Yes of course Equality is the ending of that statement Ms. Lexington"

Ms. Lexington: "Yes, correct Ms. Chasten, now for the ultimate of the whole statement Ms. Maronii can you answer Why is listening, being observant when finding the truth, justice and equality important in the world out there...?"

She stands in front of the classroom and stares dead at me, everyone turns around including Rebecca hoping that I choke, but she obviously did not know who I was still.

"It is important out there in the world where the lies hide the truth and the truth is put away from all so justice fails, equality fails so the system fails."

"Good, Good. Maronii what else..."

"It's also Important out there, because if wanting to discover all of these things you must be wise, be observant and listen carefully so you can find the truth surface the liars and justice can prevail equality can be for all and the truth can be seen in the light."

"EXCELLENT, MARONII, EXCELLENT, You have been listening very well, very well indeed. I see a great future for you, definitely if you use everything you just said. Lovely! Now can you answer the last of this statement, why is it not so important in here when applying it to my rules?"

"Because it is your rules, you set them to show boundaries and to show that in the real world like mentioned there are rules and consequences and if one should fail to follow they will fall short every time, but by the rules being your own you could have still marked me absent and locked me out, because you are the government we are just merely the people."

"Really, good Maronii, only one thing to remember about what Maronii just said class... She said I am the government and you are just the people, but without the people there could be no GOVERNEMENT."

"That's class for today; make sure that you work on your Truth vs. Lies presentation that is to be given to me on Monday morning. 5,000 words and a cover page and an entry brief to your discovery of the truth and the lies. Make sure that you use the real world... No time for imaginary worlds where we will not be able to see them so they do not what class...."

The class screams...EXIST WITHIN THESE WALLS!

"Excellent have a great weekend and see you guys at the Masquerade Ball Saturday night. GOODBYE!"

I walk up to Ms. Lexington's desk and ask her if she had heard anything about what happened on Midas? She stopped packing her briefcase and looked at me then continued<

"Now, now Maronii the Journalist, hmm I see that you have acquired a new story huh?"

"Well sort of, I just wanted to know what the heck was going on. It was crazy last night and no one seems to know anything, but everyone is whispering."

'What's the first rule of Journalism Maronii? The first rule..."

"Whispers are an imagination that we use to start assumptions that lead to rumors, so therefore the truth cannot be defined because everyone in their eyes are holding the truth, but there is no source from which it stems, so therefore once more it is not a fact, so it cannot be the truth, so it cannot be defined as justice, or equality because it has no source of truth."

"Exactly, why do you think that is?"

"Because if they are whispering that means they are also trying to find the truth within the person's whispered to and within what they think they already know."

"Correct again!"

She grabs her briefcase and heads out the classroom, I follow her and continue to talk, she continues to lecture and make me aware of the rules within the game I seek to play. Saying...

"You can have all the pieces and still be way behind the game, when it comes to using the pieces handed to you. Don't pay so much attention to the fact that your winning, focus on the little things, listen, observe and be precise. A loser can sometimes be a winner depending on how they play the game."

Then ending that lecture she says the most important...

"You cannot follow something that will lead you back to lies, Maronii do you understand?"

"Yes, Ms. Lexington"

Walking down the hall I bump into a young girl with red hair with black highlights, she was clinching her books tightly with her head down. Thank GOD I had my back pack across my chest for it would have fallen. I turned around to look back at the girl she just kept walking then for an instance she glanced back and then hurries along.

Ms. Lexington stops and say's...

"Come on Maronii if you want to hear what I got to say."

I turn around looking at the floor I see a piece of paper reading "Tammy D—" the paper was ripped so I couldn't see the rest of the name, but I knew it belonged to the girl I just bumped into. I fold the paper and put it in my Reporter Pad. I hurried back to Ms. Lexington and she continued to lecture me. Eventually we ended up at her office; she sits her things down and tells me to sit.

Ms. Lexington the Night Owl: Chapter 5

"So Maronii, you want to know of Stacy Dugal?"

I never said Stacy Dugal, how did she know? This was going to be interesting thank GOD; my next class didn't start until 3pm, so I had much time to kill with Ms. Lexington.

"How-"

She cuts me off. She was really good at doing that.

"Don't worry about how, I knew that was your interest, the question should be... Why is Stacy Dugal Missing?"

"I didn't know she was officially missing..."

"Well Maronii, you have been an AAP Journalist for what 3 years now, you know there is nothing usual about journalism and more than anything there is nothing usual about journalism at Hawkins. Is there?"

"You're right about that, Ms. Lexington."

"Would you like some tea, or juice Maronii?"

"No, thank you. So what am I not looking at that I should be?"

"Well first you should speak to anyone who is in the same dorm as Stacy Dugal, which means staff as well as students."

I take down my notes and continue to listen.

"Then you need to see did Stacy have any issues in classes or stood out more than the others within her dorm and class and any recreational. You basically have to—."

I cut Ms. Lexington off and say... "I have to get into her life all together"

"I told you I see a bright future for you Maronii, now if you're going to dance this dance you will need to remember... "When searching for the truth within a closed room all you have is what you know and what's left to find, no matter the size of the room if you know what you're looking for it will show regardless of space or time."

"Yes ma'am, so what do you know of what happened on Midas?"

"Well this is what I came into just being casual and not looking for it. You understand. Now you already know anything I say can be put on record, but it cannot come out until what..."

"Until the police have completed their investigation or circumstances have changed"

"Good girl. So basically this is what you must know first, I Know Stacy Dugal?"

I just look at her with this confusing look and I say what? Why would you know a freshman?

"Well first stop looking at me like I just told you I murdered my cat or something and two, I know her because I do the orientation for all the newbie's."

"Oh yeah that is right, I forgot, but still why do you know her, know her?"

Here it goes...

Ms. Lexington: "Well, when I first met her I didn't know who she was. It didn't dawn on me that she was the late descendant of the Founders of this Institution until Martha Peters the Astronomy teacher made me aware of it one day in the teacher's hall..."

"Wait a minute you mean Stacy Dugal, is Descendant from Penelope and Charles Hawkins?"

I couldn't believe it, I just couldn't believe it. That's why when I heard her name about a week ago, for freshman advisory picks it made me wonder. But I didn't know what to wonder about.

"Yea, so I started looking back through some old school history and come to find out, a descendant from the Dugal family has always went to this school. At first it was the Hawkins they carried that name for about 30-50 years, then eventually it carried on to Bellon, then to Ferris, then to Dugal this was all over 100 or so years ago. So looking further till when the school was founded, in 1910 the Father of all of these grandchildren and children Charles Hawkins was an alleged Adulterer and wildly known for going to Sugar Shacks, back then they were called that because of the African American maids and some still owned slaves. He would go there for the women. He was a drunk, but rich and white and very powerful, he built this town from the ground up...."

"Wow, I didn't know all of that."

I couldn't help, but to think that there was going to be something bigger here than I thought.

"His family struck oil in that day so Hawkins lived well and took over for his daddy once he passed. Soon after I think around 1910 he married a Penelope Jessop who became Penelope Hawkins, they had 6 children and so on. Well no later than that Hawkins ended up disappearing. His wife started a school, for girls and ended up dying from yellow fever so they say, after that no one knows. The kids and so on started the Masquerade ball, but it used to be called the Hawkins

Devil Dance during Halloween, but some unknown deaths occurred and no one wanted to participate in anything called the Devils Dance so they changed it to the Masquerade Ball…"

"Are you freaking kidding me this is huge. So huge"

I jumped up and walked around flipping through these notes this was just a lot to take in. Could there be a curse; could there really be a secret Hawkins family curse here? I thought about it walking around Ms. Lexington's office and I even wrote it down and underlined, until my paper got thin in that one place.

"Okay calm down Maronii, don't go and do anything crazy with what I have told you okay?"

"Yes, of course Ms. Lexington I have two questions thought you could do me the favor of answering them?"

"Yes, there couldn't be any worse than the things I already told you…"

1. "Who were the unknown deaths? The people who died here."
2. "How do you know Stacy Dugal? And the commotion on Midas last Night?"

"That's 3 questions Maronii, but okay."

"The deaths were, let me go through my notes I got here.... Wait a second…"

"So Ms. Lexington..."

She was scrambling around through books and papers and drawers trying to find the notes she had taken.

"Were any of them, Hawkins Descendants?"

She stopped scrambling and fell back in her chair....

"Yes! How did you know that?"

"I didn't it was just a guess. What's the first rule in Journalism Ms. Lexington?"

I looked over at her from the window, "SO WHAT IS THE FIRST RULE" She stared back at me with this draining look, a look that scared even me. She seemed to lose thought.

"It's...Hidden truths are only hidden if there is nothing pointing to where there hidden, therefore the truth can be found and should be found left in the right hands it will be found and brought into the light from which it has been hidden from all to see."

"Correct Ms. Lexington."

She pulled out one drawer and said...

"I put the paper in here, but now they're gone."

"What, gone? How can that be? Was anyone in your office or this part of the building when you found all of this Ms. Lexington?"

SHE LOOKED SCARED AND NERVOUS; SHE WAS RUNNING HER HANDS OVER HER FACE, AND BREATHING HARD...

"Yes, yes some girl, she had red something I can't remember. Leave this alone Maronii."

I began walking away, back to the window thinking of the girl I bumped in the hall, whose name was "Tammy D." then all the sudden Ms. Lexington screamed my name...

"CARMEN Dammit, listen to me."

"What, Ms. Lexington what is it...?"

"Don't play with the dark secrets of a hidden truth from which you know nothing of its source. It can only bring you back to more hidden truths that will be looked at by all to see as lies leave this alone Maronii!"

"Ms. Lexington in class today you said listen, be observant, and justice, equality shall prevail and be for all and the truth will be seen in the light from which it was hidden from. Now you are telling me to ignore that, I can't I just can't."

She fell back in her seat then said...

"Well take this with you...you will need it..."

It was the history book of Medico, Alabama.

"Thank you, Ms. Lexington I got to go, but I will see you soon."

I left out of her office, put the book away I didn't need anyone knowing or even hinting at the idea I was up to something. But that was my problem by past investigating everyone knew that when something happened on campus of this magnitude Maronii was going to be investigating it. I wanted to find out who was this Tammy girl that bumped me and what was she might of doing around Ms. Lexington's office. But then I had a thought Ms. Lexington never told me how she knew Stacy Dugal. So I hurried backed to her office, because there was a reason she told me all of this I just had to know why.

By time I got to her office Ms. Lexington was hanging outside her window, every kid outside was screaming and running, and administration was rushing to Ms. Lexington's office to try and save her. I just gasped and cried then I ran. What the hell was going on, I just left her not even 5 minutes and now she was possibly dead, I got to go find Peninsky I must see those pictures. <

I am not sure if Peninsky is going to like what I am going to have to say, but something is telling me he might have a small idea and if he doesn't I know who might...Megan Parex Senior Journalist she did a piece on the Masquerade Ball of 1950, was she covering up or did she just not find what I did? I don't know, but I know that she is going to be interested in this story. Next I need to get a hold of Amy my co-journalist me and her do 2 team pieces together all the time, but this one was strictly solo, but I still needed her expertise in this.

I'm running so fast I didn't even notice that I had a class beginning in 10 minutes. Instead of running over to my dorm to see if Amy might still be there until her 4pm class, I ended up having to turn back around and head in another direction before I was late for Photo-journalism with Mr. Hammond. Coming to a stop when approached by 2 campus security officers changed my whole course of direction, no Photo-Journalism today. I already knew why they were coming to get me I just didn't think it would be so quick.

I had people on campus who didn't like me and soon I would have people on the boys campus to who didn't like me, but journalism is about truth and whatever I can do to help the truth grow like a plant needing water and proper treatment I shall do, even if that means me being put right in front of a Murder investigation.

Death of Ms. Lexington First Suspect Carmen Maronii: Chapter 6

Coming to the Dean's office was a trip I didn't have a problem making, when it came to interviews or photos or even when I was elected for the Dean's list only twice so far, but I'm trying to make it a third I don't know how much this will help my chances. Looking at the clock on the wall outside of the dean's office it said 3:05pm. That was a straight up absent for Mr. Hammond and wait until he finds out the reason, "Aye, Mr. Hammond I missed your class because I am suspected of killing one of your Faculty members, but here's my homework." Hell no, that wasn't going to work I was just going to have to ride this bus all the way to What-ever-Ville before any light shed truth on anything around here even for little old Carmen Maronii.

Sheesh! I am just in it today, but I played dirty before got to get your hands dirty a little, but this was just plain messy. The security officers pushed me into Dean Lily's office and slammed the door behind me. There were 2 detectives how obvious is that, and the Dean and my dorm counselor Margret Del. She was a real SOB, one time she kicked me out of gym because I was popping gum, whoever thought Gum, really? The dean turned around and she didn't look happy at all, she told me to sit, and I did just that. One of the officers came over and proceeded to ask me questions... I just thought I would save everyone the trouble...

Death of Ms. Lexington;

"Okay, I know why I am here, I don't need to know your name or even your questions I am going to tell you the truth and that's, that. One I did not kill Ms. Lexington, and two I was in her office discussing my presentation that is or was due on Monday on the truth vs. lies in the real world. She was giving me a lecture and tips on good journalism and how to keep the clarity and originality in my work; you see I am an inspiring journalist. The Dean can tell you."

I pointed to the Dean, she nodded at the Detectives and they looked back at me, and said continue...

"So I sat in there with her for a bit listened and then left, after I left out of her office I noticed that I left something in her office so I went back, when I returned she was hanging outside her window. And that's when you guys came."

Detective Michaels: "Okay, Maronii..."

"You, officer can call me Carmen"

Detective Michaels: "Okay Carmen, so you were there to discuss as you say your presentation, and you were just there for a bit. Did you have anything to drink while you were there?"

"No, she offered me some tea or juice, but I wasn't thirsty so I declined the offer."

DM: "Okay, so when we run prints on this soda can yours will not be on here?"

"Correct, I never had anything to drink with Ms. Lexington today or for that matter any other days. And what do me having a drink with my instructor have to do with the fact that she was hanging outside her office window."

The dean looked at me and then she sat down, and began to say...

Dean Lily: "Maronii, answer these gentlemen's questions so you can get to class. Stop being a sass mouth you hear me."

"Yes ma'am."
Then out of nowhere Ms. Margret Del, had something to say.

Margret Del: "I told you dean she is a trouble maker."

Dean Lily: "Ms. Del why don't you leave that judgment up to me okay?"

Margret Del: "Of course yes ma'am!"

The next detective comes over and starts talking...

Detective Sully: "The reason it's important because we're trying to figure out just that Carmen, why a sane and young, beautiful teacher would hang herself outside her office. It doesn't make sense and not to long after you were done visiting her. And when we come to the scene we see a drink and papers everywhere. Wouldn't you ask that question?"

"Yes, I would, but once again I did not have anything to drink."

DS: "Well did you bring anything to drink? Did she seem on edge when you were talking with her?"

"I just said to your partner Mr. Sully she offered me the drinks, I declined them. What don't you understand? No she didn't seem on edge, she seemed as usual—or as normal as she has ever been when seeing her. And for the record I have visited Ms. Lexington many of times in her office, playing chess talking about modern journalism listening to Beethoven and picking her brain for all she knew. Way before this day and she has been fine every time I have left her."

DS: "Okay, Carmen I will put that on the record. One more question?"

"Go ahead shoot..."

DS: "What did you leave in the office?"

"What?"

DS: "You said hmm, give me your notepad Detective Michaels... [He flips through the other guys notes and then says] you said that you left, but then you realized you left something in her office so you went back. What was the thing you left?"

"Oh boy, I didn't plan that one, I could tell them about the book...but I could say I left my back pack. I don't know, think Carmen, think... I could say I left a piece of paper and just pull something out my bag."

"I left my graded essay paper, and I needed it to look over for my upcoming presentation."

DS: "Hmm? Okay. [He turns around and stops] can we see this essay."

"Huh?"

DS: "Can we see this essay, your dean was telling us how you're such a good writer and journalist, do you mind if we see the paper."

"Well, I really don't like my grade so I would prefer not to show it."

Margret Del: "Get out the paper, Carmen"

The dean looked at me with dead eyes and both detectives had smirks on their face. I had to pull this off, let's just hope I got that paper in my bag still she gave us that paper back a week ago.

"Yes, here it is..."

DS/DM: "Okay, you can go Carmen, but stick around we will need to talk with you again."

"Where am I going to go, I live here."

I left out of the office and shut the door; Ms. Del seemed so pissed because she just knew she was going to give it to me, but nope. I didn't do anything wrong and I wasn't going to give her or anyone the satisfaction of saying I did. I immediately rush over to the Hawkins Activities Lab, hoping I would see Peninsky, or Amy or even Megan. But I came up short on all three, but something that did peak my interest was Celine Norman, she was roaming around the activities lab, funny thing I never have seen her before in this building. This building was only for Junior and seniors, she was way out of place...

"Lost are you?"

She laughs a little then looks as if I caught her in something.

"Yes, Yes I am I was looking for a bathroom and the gym was locked so this was the nearest building so I decided to stop in here to use the activities lab bathroom."

"Oh really, I laugh and chuckle sarcastically] well crazy thing about gym, they give you uniforms where is yours? And even funnier crazy little thing about signs there's one for almost everything, like that bathroom right there that says big in black and blue letters BATHROOM not even 10 ft. away from you and I, and the really, really funny one you're going to love this, What is the odds that you would stop in the building that the reporter who interviewed you last night on the record works in? That's funny right!"

I laughed loud and so obnoxious she just stood right there and looked so guilty.

"So let's cut to the chase Celine. What the hell are you doing on the 5tth floor, my floor the journalist floor?"

She relaxed her face and closed her eyes and said...

"I was looking for you, okay, you caught me..."

"Okay, I caught you, but why were you looking for me?"

"I wanted to see if I could talk to you about Stacy, I wasn't able to tell you the rest last night because of the security officer, but now I can. Is that okay with you?"

"Hmm talk huh? Well let's go around here to my desk and you can talk on the record all you want."

"That's what I want I want it to be all on the record..."

She seemed even more anxious than last night, this girl was not right and I was pretty sure that she came to spread lies and she really believed that I was that stupid.

"So go ahead I'm listening..."

Celine Norman part 2: "Well last night I told you that, when I came up to our room, I didn't see Stacy, well the truth is she has been out of the room, almost every night this week so honestly when I didn't see her It didn't worry me. It wasn't until I seen blood on her bed that I knew there was some type of problem."

"Okay, Celine you seen blood on the bed? Stacy has been a late night creeper for every night this week? And you didn't see this as important to tell the cops?"

"Well I initially thought that she would come back, but when all the cops came I knew it was bad."

"What happened to this blood on the bed?"

"I and another girl got rid of it. I can't tell you where."

"What are you serious? You have evidence that could help find Stacy Dugal and your sitting on it like a chicken laying an egg. You must tell someone if you don't I will."

"No you won't Maronii funny thing about on the record all you have are notes, you don't have any recorder or video. So it's like I never said it and you made it all up just to get the Senior Seat."

"What, you can't be serious? You need to go, right now! Go!!"

"I will go, but none of this better come out. Or you'll be sorry!"

I throw my pin down and just laugh to myself; this day couldn't get any worse for me. Suspected of killing one of the best teachers/friends I have ever met in my lifetime and then have a prime source come and play liar, liar whose pants on fire, all I could do was laugh out loud, because Ms. Lexington would say what's the first rule of Journalism Maronii? And I would answer saying..."No source is as good as the proof you have making them a source".

Even from the underworld Ms. Lexington was still teaching me a vital lesson that I let slip, because of me wanting to find the truth behind this story so bad, and that was "Just because your eyes are open, doesn't mean you are seeing the truth in front of you, even the plainest things can be kept from sight, your job is to separate the plainest things and the lies that are keeping you from seeing in front of you."

What was I not seeing, Celine just came in here with this story, but I don't even think it was the truth. She just seemed too eager to see me, like she is stringing me along or something. Right now I am going to have to X Celine Norman off my Source's list, until I have enough to prove she is a reliable or factual source. I think now I was just going to have to look for another source in the most unlikely of places. Why was this Medico, Alabama History Book the last thing Ms. Lexington gave to me before her death?...

Medico, Alabama History Book: Chapter 7 "History of an unknown settlement that leads to a great City"

I began flipping through the book, while I sat at my desk. The cover said "Medico, Alabama History of an unknown settlement that leads to a great City" whatever that was supposed to mean. I began flipping through the pages when a piece of paper slipped out. It read "Henry Hawkins, London Bellon, Patrick Ferris, Tricia Bellon, Elaine Ferris Mary Dugal and a Robert Dugal" with a set of two different types of numbers beside them ages and years of their death. I remembered Ms. Lexington said that she had the list of people who died here that were descendants I am thinking this list is just that. I started to look at the list...

Names-Ages-Years Died
Henry Hawkins-23-1940
London Bellon-19-1950
Patrick Ferris-21-1960
Tricia Bellon-18-1952
Elaine Ferris-27-?
Mary Dugal-18-1982
Robert Dugal-24-1985

Looking at this list I couldn't help but to notice that these siblings died very young and they had died on random years and they were all in different grade levels. This is just crazy; it's like that something had to occur for them to die. And I also noticed that all the men that died were in there early twenties when here at Hawkins. All the girls were young they couldn't have been no higher than a freshman except one, which was highlighted "Elaine Ferris she didn't have a year of death, was it possible she could still be alive and if so where the hell is she? What the hell, was going on here. I stopped reading when I heard a door close; put the book back in my bag and the list in my pad.

"Whose there I yell!"

"Megan Parex: Well nice to see you to, Maronii"

"It was Megan Parex; boy was I happy to see her."

"Hey, Megan How's it hanging?"

"Good, I have a request of you, Ms. Carmen..."

"Oh boy what is it; anytime you say my government I know it's something regarding my work or work period. Hit me with it."

She laughs and stops by the file cabinet and says...

"So tonight I wanted to know if you could do some overlooking on the "Angry Journalist" article that you are working on for Friday's Column. Basically to make sure there are no errors or anything that would be red flagged as inappropriate by the dean. You get me Maronii?"

She laughs and keeps biting her carrot, takes a seat at her desk and begins to flip through a stack of papers. I just stare and try to figure out how to interview her without literally interviewing her.

"Are you okay, you look a little pale Maronii?"

I am all flustered I am trying to not look obvious, but before I knew it I was blurting out the first thing on my mind...

"So was there any hidden scandal when you did the piece on the Masquerade Ball of 1950?"

She looked at me then placed her carrot in the trash and stopped going through the papers on her desk.

"Why would you ask a thing like that Maronii? But no, there was not and if there was or is I wish to not disturb old secrets. Understand?"

"Yes, of course no, no I was just wondering because I know the Masquerade Ball is Saturday and I know you did a piece on it, just wondered if there was something else to it. But I totally got you. "

I looked at my watch and it was 6pm, I grabbed my stuff and began heading out the door.

"I will see you later okay."

"Don't forget need you in here tonight working on your article, because Maronii...Maronii..."

"Yes, yeah I'm here, article look at it, no errors or problems, got you."

"No, if it is not on my desk in the ready to be printed folder. It will not go to the printers and you will not receive a credit for this assignment and I will have to put you on probation and that will force your seat as junior journalist to be up for grabs, because that will drop you to a D, you have a B, right now, this article is your breaking into the spring article so you must have it. Do you hear me?"

I just stand there and try to put all this together what am I going to do, I have to finish this article and let me just be honest, it is a little out there, so I have no clue what I am going to do.

"Okay, no problem, I will see you in the morning."

I rush out of the building and go to the Students library, so I can continue to read this book and look up some of these people on the web or in this book. I cross through the Hawkins London Bridge which is connected to the student library... Now I understand why this is called the London Bridge, London Bellon one of the descendants who died here. Stuff was starting to make a lot of sense I tell you. What was really on my mind walking to the library was the fact I am going to have to come up with a totally different Angry Journalist article just so I will receive my credit. I get to the library pick a secluded area with a full table just for me and I bring out my laptop and put the book on the table.

I began surfing the search engine "Triangle", I start searching for "Hawkins School deaths". It didn't shock me when nothing came up. Looking through the search results there was a little article on an Elaine Ferris. Why does that name sound familiar... I began flipping through my notes and there it was, Ms. Lexington Mentioned that the names for Hawkins descendants transitioned from Hawkins. Bellon, Ferris and Dugal, I went back to the list of names from Ms. Lexington's book and there it was... "Elaine Ferris no year of death and her name was highlighted, Ms. Lexington was onto something. Now I am really starting to believe her death was no coincidence or an accident in no shape form or fashion.

I took down some notes on what I found and began to make a connective gram. A connective gram for anyone who does not know what that it is a big web of anything and everything that is relative to each other. I click on the article about Elaine Ferris...the article read...

"The Medico Journal

March 5, 1970

Suicidal Hawkins Air

An Elaine Ferris the late great Charles Hawkins Great-Great-Great Granddaughter and her husband were found in there Medico, Estate at 10pm on March 5, 1970 shot. Leonard Ferris was shot one time to the head with a hunting rifle. The cops later found Elaine Ferris in their kitchen at the dining table with one gunshot to the head as well. The cops and paramedics assumed Elaine Ferris, was dead along with her husband, but when removing her body from the crime scene she began to breathe the paramedics immediately rushed her to the Medico, county Memorial where Elaine Ferris Survived her gunshot to the head.

Later the cops ruled the death of her husband murder and the attempt on Ms. Ferris's life was considered suicide attempt after killing her beloved husband. The cops and District attorney Hilary Norman had no problems building a case against Ms. Ferris a jury of her peers found her guilty and a psychiatrist from Medico the Criminally Insane found Ms. Ferris not competent for trial. The psychiatrist Tobin Mason said that Elaine Ferris kept insisting she did not kill her husband, that something else did, but she did try to kill herself before that something got her. With no more a due the Judge found Elaine Ferris legally insane and sentenced her to life in the Medico Institution for the criminally insane.

Elaine Ferris's estate and all assets were relinquished to the county and the Hawkins school for Girls and Boys. All her assets were estimated at a total of 5 million dollars and possibly more. One thing that will never be answered... Did Elaine really have someone coming after her and if so who was it and why did they or more rather it, kill her husband and make her shoot herself. Good Day Medico!!

Kevin Holler -The Medico Journal"

Looking over the article it just blew me even more than figuring out the London Bridge was named after a dead Hawkins air. I hurried and printed off the article and then began to look over the book, maybe I would see something on the others that were on the list. I run through the pages and I come across a folded page, it read "Henry Hawkins age 23, started the train system in Medico, Alabama." I flipped some more pages and came across London and Tricia Bellon they both were sisters and they invested in the schools in the area as well as the court system here in Medico.

The most weird thing about this is that for Medico to be so small it seems to have more secrets than any other place I have been to and or lived, and I am from Sedarsville, Alabama so this is really crazy to me. I began to flip through some more, when I received an instant message on my school account from Peninsky...

Instant Message:
Penin_sky89: Hey girl, where are you?
CMaronii_thejournalist: it's not 8 already is it?
Penin_sky89: It's 7:45pm. And the building is already shut down, bring your butt.
CMaronii_thejournalist: okay I am on my way! Outcha!
Penin_sky89: Outcha!
LOGGED OUT!

Well it looks like this mystery is going to become more or less once I go through these photos with Peninsky. I start packing up my books and everything when I see that girl that bumped me in the hall, Tammy D----... I began walking over towards her she was sitting at a table by herself, with like a dozen books.

"Hey are you Tammy?"

"Who wants to know?"

"Well I am Carmen and I accidentally bumped into you today, I just wanted to apologize. I am sorry!"

"She looked up at me and to my surprise she was actually a pretty girl it's like something bad happened to her that made her go into Goth mode."

"Well, I forgive you now can you leave me alone..."

"I'm sorry to intrude I just wanted to apologize for my carelessness earlier."

I began to walk off when I noticed she was reading "Medico, Alabama History book an unknown settlement leads to a great city". What the hell, I turned around and sat back down, by now Peninsky was blowing up my phone in texts. I texted him "on my way damn" and then approached Tammy again.

"So Tammy D--- is it? Well I would like to know what interest you have in Medico history."

She looked up and started to look around.

"I'm right here Tammy D--- no need to look anywhere else, are you going to ignore me and force me to sit right here with you until you leave or are you going to answer the question?"

"I-I-I just wanted to know about the history that's all."

"Yeah I bet. So have you been in the Education Building at all before today?"

"No, why-why-why would you ask me that?"

Her stuttering just made this more interesting and official that this Tammy knew a lot. I was about to ask her about Stacy Dugal when Celine Norman came up to the table and placed her hand on Tammy's back. Tammy began to look nervous and even worried and scared. Hmm! Celine seem to be at a lot of places today looks like she is covering her basis if you ask me.

"What's up Tammy girl and Maronii"

"I was just leaving nice to see you are making your pit stops before cleaning house Celine."

"Don't you worry Maronii I won't forget to visit you again...? You ready to go Tammy?"

Celine packed up all Tammy's books and grabbed Tammy by her arm then walked off. The look in Tammy's eyes were worse than anything I have ever seen, they were sad and lonely and even more scared. I rushed over to the Hawkins Activities Lab and head to the Photo-Lab in the basement. Peninsky was sitting there with his headphones and dancing, I could almost laugh until I noticed that he had some of the pictures up and what I saw made this investigation worse than I could ever imagine.

Stacy Dugal, Tammy D--, Celine Norman and Lisa Fredrick's: Chapter 8

Walking into the Photo-Lab I see pictures of Stacy and Tammy D on the field during the staff vs. students soccer play-offs and then I see another with Celine and Tammy D—in one picture while Celine is pointing at Stacy, and another shows Stacy sitting alone at one of the banquets looking over at Celine, Tammy and Lisa. And last, but not least One shows a shadow behind Stacy and Tammy D---. What was that, and what the hell was going on? Peninsky turns around and says...

"About time girl I was about to put all these back up."

"Sorry, I have had a crazy day you would not believe."

"Okay, well just to let you know I already heard about Ms. Lexington and yes I heard you were questioned. Chick what the hell is going on, it just seems like-e-e, never mind..."

"What Peninsky, what"

"I was just going to say it is like ever since this Stacy Dugal girl has been missing shit has just been funny around here and now you were questioned about a murder. Girl something or someone doesn't want you waking up old bones I am trying to tell you Maronii leave this story on the shelves I'm telling you."

For the first time, everything that Peninsky said wasn't a plea to run or cry for attention or just being obvious. It was like even he knew stuff just was not right around here after Wednesday.

"You know you're right, but you also know I am too far into this now to just shelve it."

"Yeah, I kind of figured you were going to say that, that's why I have these pictures up so you can go ahead and do whatever it is that you do."

"Thank you, boo. First things first what is this shadow behind Tammy D—and Stacy Dugal?"

"Tammy D. Why you call her that?"

"Because I don't know her full name, I found it on a piece of paper when she bumped me in the hall and ever since then I have been trying to figure out who the hell she is."

"That's easy I know her, she helps out in the Year book club when it's time for people to place their orders for books."

"What? You know her, what the hell. Who is she Peninsky?"

"Girl that is Tammy Dugal"

"What?"

I just had this dumb look on my face like you can't be serious. All day this girl has been in my face and I had no clue and no one even bothered to tell me. I have to find Tammy before Saturday, because if anything was a fact it was that she is the key to this whole situation. If anybody knew what happened to Stacy Dugal it would be her own sister.

"Peninsky, I am going to have to cut our rendezvous short I must go find Tammy Dugal.

Why, Maronii what are you up to?"

"This is the girl I bumped into earlier. I just didn't know she was Stacy Dugal's Sister."

Peninsky looked at me with amazement, but a little confused on why she was so important to me right now to find.

"I can't explain all right now. Can I get these pictures?"

"Well, wait Maronii I didn't tell you what that shadow was."

"It's okay I will see you tonight my dorm at 11pm sharp Peninsky, if I am not there use my key to get in and wait do not let anyone in, I will knock on the door 4 times and say "C.Maronii the journalist" to let you know it's me. Be safe and do not trust anyone okay. I can't explain just please follow my instructions to the t."

"Carmen WAIT!"

I rushed out of the photo lab and I hurried to the Freshman Dorm to see if I could find Tammy Dugal. When approaching Midas Rowe I seen Celine, Lisa Fredrick's outside sitting on the bench.

"Celine where is Tammy D."

I was about to let on that I knew who she was, but I just said Tammy.

"Oh she is gone somewhere I am not sure.... Girls are going to do what they want regardless of restriction or consequences right."

It hit me like a gust of hot air, Celine has been playing this from the beginning and Tammy, Stacy and even Ms. Lexington were all a pawn. Now she thinks she has me running or scared if anything I am just mad, furiously mad. But I cannot show her that.

"Yeah, you're right Celine we are going to do what we want. Your Great Grandmother is Hilary Norman right?"

The look on her face was unbelievable; she sat up and told Lisa to leave. Lisa got up and left, she looked back and forth between Celine and me.

What you want Maronii?

I don't want anything Celine I just needed to confirm that you were who I thought you were. And you just did, good night!

I began to walk off and she screams...

Where did you find that out from? Tell me so help me...

[I turn around put my hands in my pockets and say...]

So help you what Celine, you don't scare me and one thing for sure you don't fool me. You know more and with the right sense in me I know that you had dealings in the disappearance of Stacy Dugal.

I proceeded to walk away again, and that's when she began to break...

Wait, Carmen, wait. Let me talk to you on the record all rights yours I promise.

No thank you, I am no longer interested in what lies your mouth will tell now. I tried to listen and you insisted on making up and throwing balls and playing ridiculous games. So I have a M11 flash for you Celine the truth is in line with justice and equality and somewhere in the game you are way over your head. It has taken you whole so peace for you has left your side, the only thing I care about is getting to the truth and finding what happened to Stacy Dugal. Dead or Alive I will find her. But you, you will forever be burdened with this; this moment these words and so will your children. Get in your dorm, your curfew started 5 minutes ago. Now get out my face.

She turns around and begins walking into her dorm saying...

Maronii, your right I will be burdened, but you will never find Stacy Dugal and if Hawkins is still in control you will never find Tammy Dugal neither. You're right we have nothing else to discuss.

I stand there under the street light with my hands in my pocket and I look around, and there I see Lisa Fredrick's in the window. It's a possibility that she has been there the whole time, but none of that mattered because she is just as guilty as Celine. She just doesn't know I know. I had to find Elaine Ferris and I had to do it quick. I head back to my dorm room, hoping Peninsky was in there.

"KNOCK, KNOCK, and KNOCK, KNOCK-C.Maronii the journalist"...

I would just have to hope he came to the door. The door opens and it's Peninsky GOD, I had a sigh of relief and hugged him.

"Peninsky gosh I was so worried"

"Well me and you both. Maronii there is something you need to see."

"What?"

"There are 3 things... Okay well while I was waiting here for you, 1. Is I surfed the Dugal family to see if there was anything that the town had on the web."

"What you get?"

"I printed out this obituary of a Liza and John Dugal both died on the same day from a gunshot to the head."

"Are you serious? Peninsky this just keeps getting deeper, I don't have enough paper for all the facts I am getting surrounding one girl."

"Okay, well why you are sitting down, there is something else..."

O sheesh what is it...

2. "Is in the photo I showed you with the shadow... it's not just any shadow."

   "What you mean?"

   "Give me the photo Maronii. Is your door locked?"

I get the photos out from my bag and walk over to lock the door; I even close the curtains just to be safe.

"Here it is.... What do you see?"

"Look with the magnifying glass and look at the obituary..."

"I lean down with the magnifying glass and look back and forth at least 5 times between the obituary and damn me."

"It can't be Peninsky, that's impossible."

"Well believe it Carmen, your or my eyes are not lying to us...That's Stacy and Tammy Dugal'S mother."

"OMG! What the hell man!"

3. "Is Ms. Jameson was also In a picture and wait to you see this one"

I look at the picture he is showing me and there it was Ms. Jameson talking with the Ms. Lexington near a tree behind Tammy and Stacy Dugal.

What the Hell Peninsky

"Tell me what the hell is going on Maronii, and tell me now because I am freaking out unbelievably I'm scared to even leave to go to my dorm while it's dark out there."

"Okay are you ready because it's a lot."

"Just give me all the basics..."

"Sit down... "

We both sat down and I began to tell him all that I have found out today.

Is there a Hawkins Curse: Chapter 9 "Peninsky and I investigate" Part-1

The past 24 hours: "This morning I had a talk with Ms. Lexington before she killed herself and she made me aware that Stacy Dugal and now I am aware of Tammy they are Descendants from the Hawkins family. As well as since 1950 people that are descendants have been dying, the day or days leading up to the Masquerade Ball. Ms. Lexington just stumbled upon this stuff by just doing what journalists do investigating; until the truth is presented. After that talk with her I then went back because I needed a question answered and not even 5 minutes had went by and there she was dead, hanging outside her window. I was then questioned by to, Soap Opera cops, then after that I headed over to the Activities building where I ran into Celine Norman on the journalist floor snooping around.

She then decided to tell me this bull story on how Stacy was a creeper every night and she seen blood on her sheets the night she disappeared and disposed of them her and another person, which I think could be between Tammy and or Lisa Fredrick's. After that I then headed to the library to do some research on the family name Hawkins and then I came across Elaine Ferris the Great, Great, Great Granddaughter of Charles Hawkins. Doing so I read through the article that stated that she tried to kill herself and she killed her husband she stated during the 70's that something did it, that she never touched her husband. Well since then she has been in a mental asylum for the criminally insane. After that I ran into Tammy Dugal again not knowing she was a Dugal, she didn't let off much except she was reading the Medico, Alabama history book. After that I ran over to you, we looked at the photos, once you made me aware of whom Tammy was I immediately rushed over to the freshman dorm, where I came up on Celine and Lisa sitting on a bench. Celine and I had some words, where she made it very clear that I will never find Stacy Dugal and if Hawkins has it I will never find Tammy Dugal either."

Peninsky just looked at me and says...

"Well honestly Maronii it makes sense, the one thing we need to do is find this Elaine Ferris she is the only one as right now that can shed light on this."

"That's true, but we have to take what she says with a grain of salt, remember she is in the Looney bin."

"That may be true, but right now she is all we have. And am I correct when I say that according to Celine Tammy has now disappeared?"

"That's what I am saying, I have no clue; she was not there when I popped up on Celine and Lisa. And o Celine's great, great, great grandmother was Elaine Ferris's prosecutor."

"Seriously this makes sense. It really does. And the whole town knows of the "Suicidal Hawkins Air" story. They have a saying that when a woman loses her wits it's called "You've gone Ferris Crazy."

"Are you serious? Your stupid little town, is making a mockery of that woman?"

"Aye, this was before you or me. It seems a lot of this was way before you or me. So where do you want to start?"

"Let's start with finding the address for the Medico, Insane Asylum. Once we've done that we can go there first thing in the morning. But for right now I have to come up with a totally new "Angry Journalist" article for my column in tomorrow's AAP. You can stay the night here there is a sleep couch over there and in the morning we'll stop by your dorm so you can freshen up and then we'll split out. Cool?"

"Wow, a new article... What's wrong with the one you have now, I like that one. Ha, ha, ha."

"Well, I seen Megan today and she made me aware that she wanted me to come back to go through the article again to make sure that there are no errors you know the usual and to make sure it's not inappropriate. You know I have the tendency to be out there. I can't help it I must let the truth flow period."

I laugh and then head over to my lap top.

"Oh, shit I got to email her and let her know I am just going to do it here and send her the official on the AAP, site before 5 am."

"I began emailing Megan and hopefully she will let me do it here."

"Okay, do you need any help with this Maronii?"

"No, I am fine get some sleep."

"Girl, you only have to tell me once I am so tired."

"We laugh then Peninsky lay's on the couch and heads to sleep."

I began working on this new "Angry Journalist article, how the hell am I going to pull this off. Well, one thing is for sure I am a little angry now so that should help. I could change the name and just use my original at a later time. Yeah I think I will do that. I then look up at my screen and I have an Instant Message from Megan...

Instant Message:

Megan_P: So you are not going to be able to make it back to the lab are you?

CMaronii_thejournalist: No, sorry Meg, I just have a lot to do in my dorm tonight, but I am working on the article.

Megan_P: Okay, that's fine just as long as you have it in the AAP, account before 5am. Not 5am, before Maronii.

CMaronii_thejournalist: No problem. There is something else to Meg...

Megan_P: What is it?

CMaronii_thejournalist: I am going to come up with a totally new article, is that okay or do it has to be my "Angry Journalist" article?

Megan_P: Something told me that the article was going to be a little too much, so yeah go ahead that would be best we don't need any more shots from the Dean. Considering it has been made aware to me that you are investigating the Stacy Dugal story...I knew you was I just wish you would have been the first to tell me damn Maronii.

CMaronii_thejournalist: Yeah, I'm sorry I was just trying to make sure that I wanted to be the one covering the story, before I told you.

Megan_P: Okay, do what you must, but the first sign of a lawsuit please come to me. Ha, ha, ha! Good night good luck with the new article I look forward to reading it. The Angry Journalist article will be published just letting you know, just not tomorrow. Okay?

CMaronii_thejournalist: Of course I can't wait to send it to the printers. Ha, ha, ha! Night!

LOGGED OUT!!!

I get offline with Megan and begin this new Article. What name should I give it, what am I going to write about? It is our annual season first Columns so let's see... I got it..... Thanks Ms. Lexington she gave me the encouragement I needed when she said "She seen a future for me" Time is 1am; I have 3 hours to come up with the best article I have done yet. Finishing up my article it was now 3am. I read through it and fixed any problems. I cried I was touched so much by this story. Put it in an email twice and sent it to Megan on the AAP site. That was done I could now go to bed. Spring Article...

Sending ♥ from A Place Unknown...

By: Carmen Maronii

[Junior Journalist-AAP]- [Article #: HG59650]

March 5, 2010

Hello, Hawkins Girls and Gentlemen. Today you will read an article about a Man loved by his wife so much she left her home to come to him. The two together they experienced harsh times, love and a foundation that was made of Japanese Steel. This is "Sending Love from A Place Unknown"

I would like to dedicate this Article to Ms. Gina Lexington the Advanced Journalist instructor and amongst other titles, but she was and will always be the best teacher I have ever had the pleasure of learning from and forever a dear friend. R.I.P Ms. Lexington

Leslie and Martin Denver were two high school sweethearts; they first met in the 9th grade. Leslie instantly knew Martin was for her and Martin as well. The two graduated high school together and then went off to college, once done with school Leslie eventually found Martin again. By this time Martin had enlisted in the Army, going on his 1st tour in Iraq. Leslie and Martin both decided to get married to them there love was forever, eternal they were meant for each other. They got married in Montgomery, Alabama. They both were married for exactly two years before Martin went on his second tour to Iraq.

Leslie became full of grief and depression, Martin being worried about his wife requested for a week of stay to go back home to take care of her. Weeks had passed before Martin heard anything from his commanders. At this time Leslie decided that if he couldn't come to her she would go to him. She immediately purchased a plane ticket to Iraq; she got all of her passports and, vaccines. At this time Martin received his release papers, he immediately got on a plane back to Alabama. Leslie finished with all paper work got on a plane to Iraq. Martin made it home to find, Leslie was not there. He called family and friends no one knew where she had went. The cops eventually got involved they made Martin aware that she has to have been missing for 24 hours before she could be officially labeled as missing.

They waited...Hours and more hours passed still not 24. At this time Leslie was touching down in Iraq; she got in a local cab and was heading to her husband's camp. Overwhelmed with joy and her heart racing she was more alive than she has ever been. Than the worse of the worse happened, being stopped in the middle of the road by a man and a cart, waiting for the man to move a street bomb went off. She and 20 people were killed instantly. Martin at home stressed, upset and worried he has no idea where his love went. Sitting with his mother and family and in-laws Martin received a knock on the door. Opening the door he was met by his Captain and another Captain. Martin shocked to see them let them in and began to find his release papers that were approved.

They stopped him and told him "that's not why we're here son". Martin and the family relieved asked "so why are you here Captain?" It's about your wife, Martin..."What about Leslie?" I am sorry to tell you this, but she was found along many killed in a street bomb In Iraq" That cannot be Leslie would not be in Iraq," Hurt and, baffled the family began to cry and fall to their knees, Martin blaming himself ran out of the house into the middle of the street consumed by grief, was unaware a FedEx truck was coming down the street. He was hit so hard he died almost instantly. The family ran over to him... The last words ever spoken from Martin Denver "Leslie, I LOVE YOU"

Continuing Part 1... "Peninsky and I Investigating": Chapter 9

Waking up to a phone call, I look over at my clock and it was 6am, are you serious I think I just went to bed 3 hours ago. Shoot!

✆ Phone Call:

"Hello?"

"Morning, Carmen you sleep?"

"No, what's up Amy?"

"Well I thought you would like to know that there are cops on Midas."

"What?"

"Yep, and it has nothing to do with Stacy Dugal."

"Okay I'll be right over. Aye, Amy can you bring me another AAP Pad the bigger ones and meet me over there and do you know if the Paper has sent to the printer yet?"

"Okay, no problem and yeah the paper is there I am at the printers now. And let me say your Article was the best, you will def. win Article of the season with "Sending Love from A Place Unknown."

"Well, thanks. I'll see you in 10 minutes"

"Okay, Outcha!"

"Outcha!"

"CALL ENDED!!!"

I hang up and immediately and wake up Peninsky.

"Wake up Peninsky cops is over at Midas again."

"What? Again"

"Yep, that was Amy that just called and according to her it has nothing to do with Stacy Dugal"

"What----, I am just going to stop saying what the hell is going on, because when I think that I am close to the answer something like this happens and I am reminded that nothing is usual at Hawkins."

"Yep, so put on your pants and shoes I told Amy to meet us over there in 10 minutes.'

"Okay, Okay! Did you ever get the article done?"

"O, yeah sent it off twice at 3am, and according to Amy she loved it and it should take the title best Season Article for spring."

Me and Peninsky high five each other and do our little dance then run to the bathroom for some mouthwash. I grab my bag lap top and sandals and head out the door. Screaming for Peninsky to bring his, ass on, he comes rushing out behind me. We hop in my car because walking was not an option today not with the places we have to go, there were no classes for him or me so it was investigating day.

"Peninsky after we cover this we will swing you by your dorm and let you get cleaned up then we will head to Medico Insane Asylum cool."

"Cool, let's get this mystery solved partner."

We high five and make our way to Midas Rowe

"Aye, do you have the address?"

"Girl I put it in your pad last night because me being the smart one I knew something like this may happen."

We laugh and a give a sigh of relief.

"Thanks!"

"Welcome, we're good partners already."

"Better believe it."

Pulling up on Midas Rowe, we see even more cops then what I seen just Wednesday night. I and Peninsky began looking around for Amy; we point her out over near the Penelope Hawkins Statue

Amy: "Here's your pad Maronii. Hey Peninsky!"

"Peninsky: Hey, Amy."

"What's going on?"

"Well I been here for about 5 minutes and so far I seen them bring out one body."

"What? A body, whose"

"You'd never guess..."

I and Peninsky look at her like damn tell us.

"Who Amy?"

"Ms. Beverly Jameson"

Peninsky jaw drops and I look at him and say...

"Really"

Peninsky: "I am not surprised to say the least"

"Me either... So was she dead or alive"

Amy: "Well from what I could see she had blood on her head, but she was moving so I don't know."

Next we see them bringing another person out, and to my surprise this really did surprise me...It was Celine Norman in handcuffs.

"What? Did she do this?"

"Peninsky: Carmen this has taken a turn girl"

"Yeah, your right you two find some of the girls from this dorm and tell them to meet me around at the Henry Field okay."

Amy/Peninsky: "Yes of course. We're on it!"

We all run in different directions I run over to the cops that had Celine.

"Celine are you okay?"

"I didn't do it Maronii, something did, but I didn't."

I just looked at her funny, because that was the same thing Elaine Ferris said in her statement to the cops when she was arrested for supposedly killing her husband with a rifle, was Celine still playing games, could this be another string along with her, or did she not hurt Ms. Jameson.

"Come to the jail, please you must hear me out. Please Carmen!"

I just stand there, I have no clue what to do with her, but I will hear her out.

I run off to the Henry Field with my bigger AAP pad in hand. Meeting up with Amy and Peninsky and from what I could tell they had at least 30 girls at the field this was great. Including Lisa Fredrick's what the odds are of that.

Henry Field, Freshman Dorm Girls and Carmen, Amy and Peninsky...

"Okay everybody listen up"
I walk around pacing looking at who seem to be the guiltiest.

"One of your fellow roomies disappeared and now today another has been charged with attempting to kill, or hurt your counselor. Does anyone have anything to add to these puzzling situations?"

Out of nowhere I see a young girls hand go up.

"Yes, you what is your name?"

She began to open her mouth when Lisa Fredrick's come from the back and whispered something in her ear.

"I don't have anything to say."
"Lisa what are you trying to do here, If you're not going to help just leave."
"If I leave all of them will come with me."
"Do what you must but this is far from over."

Lisa gathered up all the girls and they walked off. I and Peninsky and Amy just stood there and looked at each other.

"It's okay guys, now we know there is a break in the chain we can get through this much quicker now. Remember that young girls face, because we will be seeing her again. Peninsky you ready to go."
"Yep."
Amy: "Well you guys I have to get the papers throughout all buildings I will see you later?
Maronii/Peninsky: Yes, Outcha!"
Amy: "Outcha!"

I and Peninsky head back to the car. When I saw the weirdest thing, Ms. Martha was talking with the police. That's funny considering she isn't even in that dorm. Then I remembered Ms. Lexington told me that Martha told her who, Stacy was.

Gotcha!

While driving off, I had Peninsky take a picture of Martha and The officer talking, and then we made our way to 4400 Wellingtons Lane, which was all the way on the other side of town, good thing about that it was far from Hawkins.

Medico Insane Asylum, 4400 Wellingtons Lane/Elaine Ferris: Chapter 10 "I and Peninsky Investigating" Part 2

Pulling up to 4400 Wellingtons, Lane was the scariest drive and destination I have ever taken. Peninsky lucky little Diva, fell asleep on me so it was just me and the scenery and a "Trinity-Life is a Party CD" gosh those girls can make some good music. When finally parking I beeped the horn just to wake him up in an "I'm mad that you could sleep and I couldn't type of way" He jumped up so fast he hit his face on the window, how I couldn't tell you. But I laughed so hard, I almost choked on all the words I wanted to say... HA, HA, HA.

"What the heck Carmen, do you have to be a Fish about waking me up?"

I laugh and say let's go, queen we got work to do.

"Okay, I'm up."

We both get out of the car and look up at the Building and it looked like an old run down castle, but for some reason over this castle was a dark cloud and just a sense that black was its favorite color. I don't think they get spring here, just hell's weather. It was super tall like the Statue of Liberty tall, it had all types of tree vines going up all sides of it, the windows were barred and there was a big huge wrap around drive way.

Three Asylum trucks, a big courtyard where a couple of crazies were, a pool that had no water and look liked it hadn't been cleaned in 50 years. With these long narrow steps, Peninsky and I felt like we were walking to our judgments. We made it up the steps, but we still didn't even get in the building yet we had to catch our breaths.

Peninsky: "We have to work out, because I feel like my lungs are on the ground right now, and why the hell they need all these steps."

"I can feel you on that one; my lungs are just all over the place. They have all these steps so if a crazy does want to escape they'll think twice about it before doing so, just by looking at all those damn steps."

We laugh and walk in the building

We enter through these big black and white double doors. Something really strange caught my eye, on both doors there was a sign that said "The Wicked shall, perish, if thee cannot find righteousness. Thee will be forbidden to enter heaven and shall lay forever with the devil." That was a little harsh, but that was not why I was here so to the task at hand. We walk in and immediately feel like we've stepped into another dimension, it smelled like old moth balls and a toilet stopped up with feces for months mixed with air freshener.

It just made me want to vomit. We see a lady at a desk; the desk looked about the same age as her, old, broken down and no good. Peninsky goes to sit down, he looks like he's about to vomit.

I walk up to the woman and to my left there were a set of doors that said A-M and to my right there were another set of doors that said N-Z. But either way you could not see behind them no glass window nothing. Behind the desk there were a set of steps wonder where those went with a sign that said "Doctor's chambers and Orderlies.

Lady at the Desk:

"Hello, I am Carmen Ferris; I was coming to see my grandmother, Ms. Elaine Ferris."

She opened her mouth and this annoying sound came out like she swallowed a thousand cigarettes a day, I made that conclusion when she smelled like a thousand cigarettes a day. Her teeth were decayed, breath smelled like cigarettes and then some.

"Yes, Ferris you say?"

"Yes ma'am"

Sweetie does it look like my name tag say's ma'am?

"I'm sorry, I meant to say..."

"I started staring at her tag trying to pronounce this wicked witch of the west's name and it read "Eugenist" What the hell, U-gin-ist it sounded like an organ at a church. That really just confirmed she was old way old.] Eugenist

"Okay, so are you on your grandmother's contacts or any paper work?"

"No ma--, I mean Eugenist I have been out of the state for some time and now I came back to continue my studies I thought I would pay Gammy a visit. "

"Hmm! what was your name again Hun?"

"Carmen Ferris"

"Okay Carmen, I am going to need you to fill out this visitors log and then take a seat over there and as soon as one of the orderlies comes up I will have him take you to her. When you bring the form back I will give you a couple of the old M.I.A regulations."

"M.I.A..."

"That means Medico-Insane-Asylum sweetie"

"Oh, yes of course"

I chuckle and then take the clip board over to the waiting area with Peninsky.

"Maronii---"

"No, Peninsky its Carmen Ferris and you will be Gregory Dillinger you got it."

"Oh, Lucifer girl you are lying now and you giving us alias. And why do I have to have the last name of America's most wanted."

"Did you really think I would come in here and say "Hey I am here to see Elaine Ferris I am a journalist at Hawkins School for Girls and it is possible that she really might be affected by a curse. I would like to see her" No, idiot if we're going to do this we have to be smart, because as soon as someone knows who we are and why we're here we could bring a house down with us in it. You understand?"

Peninsky: "yes, your right, I'm sorry this place just gives me the creeps."

"I understand that feeling, but we're almost there Peninsky. I am scared to, but I will see this through. I understand if you cannot."

"Girl, there is no way I am leaving you hanging, we can do this together and we will. Now grant I'm not use to investigating, but what the hell. I am too far into this now to turn around."

We laugh and give each other a hug. I finish up the sheet and take it back to the desk. Eugenist was gone and now there was this young black lady, she seemed nicer than the old hag.

"Here you go Judy"

I looked at her name tag, saved myself that embarrassment this time.

"Okay, let me see"

She flips through the 2 little sheets of paper and say's.

"Okay here are a couple of things you need to know, before I allow you to enter this facility. Please tell your friend over there to come here he must also here this..."

"Peninsky come here"

He walks up to the desk and she begins giving us the M.I.A.

"This is your orientation, your brief whatever you call it, but here it is known as the M.I.A you understand?

1. There are no wondering offs allowed
2. The doors to your left is for the women
3. The doors to your right is for the men
4. The steps leads into 5 different floors, [1-being the orderlies, 2- being the doctors, 3-5 are for the criminally insane] that is where your grandmother is.
5. You are to where these badges at all times

6. If you come into contact with a patient you must immediately find an orderly or run to your nearest Red box, the red box is labeled "Help" you push that button and immediately an orderly will find you. There are 8 security guards throughout this whole facility 2 for the men, 2 for the women and 6 for the criminally insane.
7. If you have to use the restroom make sure that you actually go to the bathroom that says "Visitors Bathroom"
8. Very important always stay with your orderly. If he leaves you in the room with whomever you're visiting [refer to rule number 1]. Look out into the hall to see if you see him if not go back in the room and close the door always. Or come into the hall and close the door and go to the red box and push the help button.
9. Any questions, ask the orderly do not keep them to yourself that could mean a difference in you getting lost or being severely hurt.
10. Never leave out through an exit door, always come back the way you came so you will end out here, those exits are connected so staff can get to a floor quicker, but not to leave the building.

Any personal belongings are your responsibility. Do you two understand?"

We say yes, and she tells us to sit back down until the orderly comes.

Peninsky: "So do you have a plan, Carmen?"

"Sort of, right now I am just leaning on being simple and not making her mad or upset. We don't want to be kicked out."

"That's true."

An orderly came up and told us to follow his.

Orderly: Benny Hampton

"So you two are here to see good ole Elaine, huh?"

"Yes, she's my grandmother"

"You can hold that lie, I don't care."

Wow, so he knew I was lying. Wondered what else he knew

"Why would you say that?"

"Because Ms. Elaine has been in this Asylum for 40 years and not once has anyone came to see her. If you were her granddaughter you would have at least been here once."

"That still doesn't mean that I could not be her granddaughter"

"That could be true if my dad hadn't worked here for 30 years and told me the story of her as well, was her most trusted orderly. She told my father everything all about the attempted suicide and the murder of Robert Ferris and most of all how she was sad she couldn't have any children."

Well, that kills that little fly again.

"Okay you're right"

"And also I know who you are"

"What do you mean?

Me and Peninsky stop and stare at each other; it felt like we were going up 200 steps just to get to the fifth floor.

"You're that journalist kid, from Hawkins."

"Why would you say that?"

"Because my little sister attends your school and she reads all your articles."

"O really, what's her name I might know her..."

"Melody"

"Ok, it doesn't sound familiar"

"Well yeah she's really not a social bug; I think that's why my parents put her in Hawkins to make her a people person."

"What do you mean Elaine couldn't have kids?"

"She can't have them I guess the pipes aren't right or whatever. But she can't have them."

Me and Peninsky stop behind that orderly.

"Why you stop?"

"We're here."

"You're not going to report us or anything?"

"Honestly, she doesn't get any company so I feel for her and she was really great to my dad and she has never been a problem for me and I have been here 3 years. So visit her, but the moment she becomes upset I will report you, both of you."

"Thank you, what's your name Hampton, Benny"

We shake each other's hands and to be honest he is so cute, and he was such a sweetheart.

"Nice to meet you Benny"

"Nice to meet you Carmen, remember when I said my sister reads your articles?"

"Yeah, what about them?"

"I read them to, and I have to say I like what I see---I mean read, I like what I read."

"Thank you Benny, maybe I will see you again and I can let you pick my brain.

[I giggle and flutter my eyes]

"I hope so; I look forward to seeing you again Carmen."

"Me to, thanks again"

"No problem, just make sure you play nice so I can see you again "

He stares me up and down and locks eyes with me, he was nice and tall gorgeous smile, well-toned and country gosh I love country, real chocolate and he looked like he could treat a girl nice.

Me and Peninsky, walk into the room, there she was the biggest piece to this puzzle. MS. ELAINE FERRIS. She had this lovely skin tone for an older woman who was confined all the time. She had long flowing golden curly hair, with the deepest southern accent I have ever heard. She reminded me of a Southern Mistress with her big plantation home and land with the white tea table and chairs on a great sunny Alabama day.

Meeting Elaine Ferris:

"Hello, Mrs. Ferris I am Carmen Maronii and this is my best friend Jacob Peninsky"

She turned around and looked at me and Peninsky then say's...

"Pa-nin-skee... Was your great grandfather a worker at the sugar mill?"

"Yes ma'am he was, you knew him."

"Yes, I did. He was a good man; it hurt me to hear that he passed not more than 20 years after me coming to this place"

"Yes ma'am he died young if you ask me"

"Well yes he did. We all were young in those days some of us wasted away with alcohol, some murder and then some fatal unexplainable deaths."

She looked off out through her window she seemed sad just thinking on those old days. But for a woman who shot herself she seemed fine and mentally stable. A part of her bottom jaw was scarred, but she aged perfectly.

"That's why I want to talk to you Ms. Ferris."

"Please call me Elaine... Ferris is no longer a part of me."

"Yes Elaine. Could I ask you some questions about the Hawkins Family?"

She stopped staring and immediately turned to me and Peninsky.

"What? No, no, leave those bones buried you hear me child. All you will do is wake up spirits that have not found any type of peace."

"I wanted to know about your story, your role in the Hawkins family, is that okay."

"There is really nothing to say really, I married Robert Ferris, he was a descendant of the Hawkins family I just married into it. Have a seat this may be a while."

"Okay that is fine with us.

[We took a seat and began to listen]

"Is it alright if I take notes?"

"Yes of course, my story is already out there. You know movie and book people have come to talk to me, but I won't see them no, no my life was a tragedy and the murder of my husband was the worse of them all. Why would I want to profit from that."

She just shook her head and then sat at the window.

Elaine Ferris Story:

"So it was the summer of 1968 me and Robert had just got a new automobile. It was exactly 3 days after we got the automobile that we received a call telling us his sister Lisa had been in a car accident. We didn't find out about the baby until we arrived at the hospital, the doctors said she could have lost her child, I and Robert immediately rushed to Medico, Memorial. When we arrived the doctors told us that she had passed, but the baby was still alive. So I and Robert decided to adopt the child. We adopted the child, at first everything was exciting and we were a very happy family...

"So Elaine, what did you name her?"

"We named her Danity after Robert's sister that was her middle name."

"Okay, and was Robert's sister a Hawkins as well?"

"No, she was actually a bastard child."

"What you mean?"

"She was conceived with another, while Charles father was out being an Adulterer, being a drunk and messing with those black women."

"Really, was this a common trait of the Hawkins men...?'

"Whatever do you mean, sweetie?"

"Well, I mean cheating and drinking?"

"Well at first it just seemed coincidental not fact, but then Robert started the same pattern..."

"Do you know of the woman Robert's father had Lisa with?"

"Sweetie that was so long ago, over 40 years... let me think..."

I and Peninsky started to link stuff together, I began making another connective gram.

"Ah, yes I got it her name was Fredrick's, a Marguerite Fredrick's"

"Fredrick's... are you sure Ms. Elaine?"

"Yes, yes child"

I and Peninsky just eyed each other.

"Did Robert have any problems with Lisa considering his father denied her?"

"No, never was it quite the opposite, they spent every second together."

It started to dawn on me that the child Elaine thought she adopted could have actually been Roberts.

"Okay, now back to my story..."

"So we adopted Lisa's child and raised her as our own. Around the end of 1968 Robert began experiencing some symptoms of depression; he would start drinking in the morning at night anytime he could. He stopped spending time with me and with Danity. At first he said that the baby reminded him of his sister then he just stopped talking. He would come in drunk and smelling of whores, I knew where he been he was down in the gutters with them women...."

"Okay I have a question, are you racist Ms. Elaine"

"No, never have. But anyone those days were down in the gutters black, white, Asian any woman. Black women African American's were no problem to me and I had no problem with them. The gutter just simply meant whore houses."

"So eventually I stopped wondering where Robert was and then March 4, 1970 he calls me and said "I will be home soon". I knew he was drunk. I had sent the baby to Lisa's mother's house; she and I had no problems with one another. I was sitting at the kitchen table when Robert came in drunk as he ever was he then proceeded to tell me a secret he had held from me for years. In the winter of 1966 I found out that I could not have children. Up until that point I and Robert tried every waking moment to have children, but once we found out our marriage really began to suffer."

"Robert at first wanted a divorce, but then he changed his mind he said that his father never divorced his mother, so he was not going to start...."

"Elaine... is Robert's father still alive?"

"Yeah he's married to Lisa's mother Marguerite now."

"What?"

"Yeah, sweetie Robert's mother died of Yellow Fever and maybe a year after her death Peter married Marguerite"

"Did you say yellow fever?"

Yes, that's what he said no one ever thought twice about it, especially Robert whatever his dad said Robert jumped and kept jumping. But that was the problem Peter was never happy. He definitely wasn't happy when Robert married a small town girl that use to work on a farm. Peter hated me more than anything, but even more he hated Robert for not listening to him. I think Robert blamed me because that night he showed it more than anything."

"Go ahead Elaine, we're listening"

By now the time was 12 noon.

"So he comes into the kitchen and takes a seat, across from me. I ask him what's going on Robert, he tells me that for now we both know our marriage was failing. That we knew that this was going to happen, I asked him what he meant. He told me that Lisa's daughter was his daughter. I got up from the table and ran towards the steps. He pushed me on the steps and told me to listen to him; I was so upset I couldn't even think straight..."

Elaine begins to cry as she relives the tragic murder of her husband.

"He stands in front of me and takes a sip of his bourbon, then tells me that it's my fault that his dad hates him and he had to conceive with Lisa. It's my fault that I can't have kids and he was going to get divorced and marry Lisa, he has always loved her, but she died. He tried to love me; he thought adopting his daughter would change how he felt, but every day after Lisa's death he was constantly reminded of her every time he looked at the baby. I pushed him away overwhelm with shame and being hurt, taking off upstairs he followed me and I kicked him down the stairs. I ran up to the room closed and locked the door; I sat in our closet crying, when I heard it..."

"What did you hear Elaine?"

"The gunshot, I ran out the closet screaming no, no, no by time I got to the living room the door was open and My Robert had a gunshot to the head. I grabbed his gun and took it with me to the kitchen I sat there with the gun in my hand and all my thoughts that's when I put it under my jaw and pulled the trigger if I knew that it wasn't going to kill me I would've just taken all the pills I had in my medicine cabinet. When the cops told me that I was being charged with murdering Robert I, told them something did it, but I didn't.... That was the truth."

"Why would you say that?"

"Because Robert wouldn't have killed himself, he was a lot of things, but he wouldn't have killed himself."

"Ms. Elaine excuse me for speaking frank, but you said that your husband was upset and drunk, isn't it possible that he could have done it?"

"No, I refuse to believe that."

"You said the door was open?"

"Yes, that is what also made me think Robert didn't kill himself. I have never stopped believing that."

"Ms. Elaine what can you tell us about the woman who prosecuted you?"

"You mean Hilary Deanna Norman...."

"How do you know her so well?"

"Well in high school I played volleyball, I also attended Hawkins. When I met Hilary Norman, she was a part of the AAC, her mother was the head of the PTA and all that crap. During this time I was simply no one important, no money, no status and no husband in the works. Hilary had everything. What you two must understand is until you understand Hawkins you will never understand any of this. That school is a big part of this, but even more so is the Family that is stems from.

So I played volleyball, Hilary played cheerleading, she was a popular, pretty mean girl everyone loved her when you have what others want it's easy for everyone around you to not see the true you. So one day there was a fundraiser event for the Kids in the ICU at Medico Memorial.

I signed up and well Norman just got it. We both were the only ones on the field to run, when it started I took off like a bullet, Hilary did to, but her shoe strings were untied so the head judge made her stop to tie them. Me knowing my speed I told her that we can start over again. They started the race over, this time we both were competing and as hard as we could, in the stands was Robert, Lucas and Neil Ferris Robert was the youngest of them they already pretty much finished school so last to go was Robert. He was so cute and talented look him up you will see he was a basketball star, football and tennis. Well they were watching me and Hilary race, I never paid any attention to Robert, but Hilary did.

She paid a lot of attention, so when she seen him in the stands she got greedy and she got vicious she ran over into my lane and pushed me. I fell behind a little, but I eventually caught up just in the nick of time and when I did she was too busy trying to push me again and when she did I slowed down and she ran into the wall. I blew through the finish and won. After that Hilary had it out for me. But when she found out I married Robert it was no surprise that she was prosecuting me in his murder."

"Wow, you have had a life Ms. Elaine"

"Yes I did. Well is that all?"

I and Peninsky look at each other.

"Ms. Elaine you sure you don't want to shed any light on the Hawkins family?"

"I told you I did not want to talk about that sweetie. That's a story that you will have to answer all on your own. But I will tell you, look within the school, look with in the town do not rule out anything until you know for sure it's not fact."

"Did you happen to take Journalism at Hawkins?"

"Yes, I had a teacher named Corona Lexington"

I and Peninsky stop from leaving out of the room.

"Lexington? Are you sure?"

"Of course, I am you think I would remember all that I just told you and not remember a teacher, foolish child."

"I ask Elaine, because yesterday my teacher Ms. Gina Lexington was found hanging outside her window after I found your name on a list of descendants of Hawkins."

She stood firm and said...

"Girl get out of here, and don't ever come back."

Then slammed the door...

Peninsky: "well what we did get from her was good though"

"Yes, but Ms. Lexington..."

We stopped talking when Ms. Elaine opened up her door and throughout a piece of paper. Peninsky picked it up while I walked to the red box.

"Carmen you aren't going to believe this."

"What is it?"

I rush back and Peninsky hands me the paper. It was a picture and on the back it said "Lexington, Ferris, Norman, Fredrick's, Jameson and Peninsky, Parex Class of 1960." I couldn't believe it all these families were connected somehow, and on the front everyone's faces, including Peninsky great, great, great grandfather.

We got to get out of here and go to the town library.

Orderly Benny Hampton came back to take us back to the lobby. I and he flirted and I gave him my cell number. Reaching the lobby, I shake Benny Hampton's hand again and tell him if he's not busy he should come to the Masquerade ball with me as my date. He hurries to say yes and I tell him to call me later and I will meet him in town.

We drop our badges off at the desk and Ms. Judy was gone now was Eugenist

"GOODBYE, You little ingrates."

"I am so irritated with this woman; I couldn't help what I did next..."

"You know what Ma'am, being rude because you're alone and you smell like an ash tray is no reason to be rude to people who are not rude to you. If you don't like your job quit and if you don't like people go to a tobacco plant. But the next time I come see my grandmother and you decide to be rude, I will just have to call Governor Baxter and let him know that you may be failing on your job of keeping the people safe while here. I think he would find it very interesting and important when he hears two teenagers were in your facility and almost got hurt and you were so busy trying to fix what's left of your hair that you didn't notice a patient walking towards you when I was exiting the building."

She looks confused and then I point to the tall white man storming towards her, lucky for her I knew two orderlies were coming down the hall, but she didn't.

"Let's go, Peninsky"

"You got it Maronii, Outcha!"

We run down the steps and laugh all the way to the car; we drive off and just feel like we crossed the Great Wall of China.

"We're headed to the Medico Library"

"Okay, what are we looking for?"

"Anything about Hawkins school and this photo...."

"I am starting to think that all of these people in the photo done something then that is catching up now, not sure how it plays with Stacy and Tammy Dugal, but we will get there."

"Okay I am going to scan the picture on my phone and send it to Charlie to see if anything is unusual or if anything is linked to it."

"That's great let me know when he gets back to you."

I receive a call from Megan

✆ Phone call:

"What's up Boss?"

"Where are you Maronii?"

"I am headed to town, what's going on?"

"Well Ms. Jameson has died, they thought she was going to make it, but she died a little while ago in the hospital.'

"What? I'll be there in 30minutes."

"Since you're going into town you might want to meet up with "me at Medico Memorial I got something to give you."

"Okay, sure make it 20m. I'll see you soon"

CALL ENDED!!!

"What's up Maronii?"

"Ms. Jameson is dead so that now makes Celine a murderer and if she tells the cops what she told me she will be where Ms. Elaine is."

"Dead! So where are we headed to now?"

"Meeting Megan at the Hospital, then after that if we don't get any more curve balls we will head to the library."

"Okay, cool. I SENT THE PICTURE OFF TO CHARLIE!"

"Great, let's hope Megan has something good."

Megan Parex and Ms. Jameson's Gift to Carmen Maronii: Chapter 11

When I and Peninsky pulled into town, we immediately looked for anything that was suspicious; we don't trust anyone anymore because it seems this whole town is hiding everything and nothing seems true to the eye anymore. We pull into the Hospitals parking garage and we see Megan sitting in her car, looking through some envelope.

"What is she looking at Maronii?"

"I have no clue, Peninsky but we do not tell her anything until I know if we can even trust her. Remember her family name was on the picture to. If she asks us where we been we will tell her out at Penelope Bridge throwing bread at the birds okay."

"Yes, I got you"

We pull up right beside Megan; we get out of the car and talk outside.

Megan:

"What's up Megan, you seem a little nervous or on edge?"

"No of course not. So what have you guys been doing?"

"Peninsky: Hanging out feeding the birds you?"

"Well, nothing much just you, know can't believe Ms. Jameson is gone"

"Yeah it's a shocker because I know I heard the paramedics say she was going to live, so what happened?"

"I don't know I just came here?"

"Really, why are you here?"

"Just hanging out like you guys"

"Okay, hmm? So what you got there?"

"O yes, yes this is what Ms. Jameson wanted me to give to you. What is it?"

"I don't know I haven't looked at it."

"Now this really made me weary of Megan now, I just saw her looking at this exact envelope, why would she lie?"

"Oh, really okay. Well I am going to head back to the dorm and I'll check you at the lab in the morning?"

"Yes, and wonderful job on the article Maronii it really did do a number on everyone. The campus is buzzing with your article. Great job!"

"Thanks, I learn from the best!"

"See you guys!"

Maronii/Peninsky: "Bye!"

Megan gets in her car and drives off, me and Peninsky drives off behind her heading to the library

"So what do you think is in this envelope Maronii?"

"I have no freaking clue Peninsky, but whatever it is, Megan seen it."

"Yes, I noticed to she lied about it. Why?"

"Because she knows something"

"Megan... no way"

"Are you still thinking that everything you knew or know is still the truth if so, you are screwed?"

"I am just saying, Maronii not everything me and you both know is a lie."

I pulled the car over to give Peninsky a reality check

"Get a grip Jacob, you have spent all day with me and you just came out of a mental ward are you seriously saying you still believe your town can do no wrong? You hold a picture in your hand with your great, great, great grandfather in line with some of this towns wealthiest families you had no clue, he even went to Hawkins. Stop! Just stop... I don't need you to be irrational, I you need to see the obvious the obvious of which your eyes will not deny you, your ears will not close on you and your hands that will continue to feel. You hold a picture, you heard Ms. Elaine, and you see all of this. If you can't do this just go back to the school and I will do it myself."

Peninsky looked at me and said...

"Maronii, this is so much to take in, I feel like we are about to dig up secrets and I am scared that my family is at the pit or top of that. What do you expect me to do?"

"I don't expect you to do anything, I just want you to be strong and be my friend. Can you do that Peninsky?"

"Yes, I can I told you that I was not going to leave you hanging and I am not."

"I and Peninsky drive off to the library. Passing Megan meeting up with Rebecca Chasten"

"Did you just see that Maronii?"

"Yes I did Peninsky, yes I did. That's why I told you what you knew before this day is no more. Just look at everything I believed and now I have to go through with a fine tooth comb. How do you think I feel?"

We pull up at the library and head in

"We will go to a secluded table I will look at what's in this envelope why you look for book's surrounding Hawkins Family. I don't care if it is Charles Hawkins or his wife we just need all we can get."

"Okay, I'll be back."

I began going through the Envelope. 3 pieces of paper fall out a ring and a journal. The pieces of paper seem to be some type of bank statements from Medico Trust. The second was this old ruby ring that had the initials MGP...Now I had to find out what the hell this was. The third thing was a journal kept by Ms. Jameson. It seems that she has kept up with this journal since the late 1950's. This could be something to our investigation. I flip through some pages and I noticed that a whole middle section has been ripped out. I play back the time i saw Megan going through the envelope, I am pretty sure she was ripping out those pages that are now surprisingly missing.

"Okay I have like 8 books here and 5 of them are about Hawkins and the other 3 are about Lexington, Parex and Jameson."

"Okay, cool sit down Peninsky, right across from me.

"Okay, why you look like something else has taken a turn for the worse.

"Well not really. Here we have some bank statements from Medico Trust and a ruby ring with the initials MGP and last but not least a journal handwritten by someone and Ms. Jameson. And also Megan ripped out like 10 pages out of this book.

"Are you serious?"

"Yes, take a look"

Peninsky looks at the book, and says...

"Maronii there is a lot of talk in here about MGP"

"It is? Let me see."

"Right there, both pages"

"I look at the pages and there it was MGP, Michael Gregory..."

"See the page is ripped so once again I have half of a name.

"Well it's better than just having MGP"

"That's true. But wait a minute you have books on all the families' right?"

"Yeah, why"

"Well maybe the initials are in one of these family books"

"Yes, yes"

"You take 4, I'll take 4."

"Okay I'll take 2 of the Hawkins and Jameson"

"I'll take Parex and 3 Hawkins and Lexington"

"Alright"

"Write down any notes that stand out, we could be here all night if we don't pay attention to detail."

"We don't want that. Let's get started..."

I get a text on my phone from an unknown number. Come to find out its Benny Hampton. I text him back. He tells me that he is off from work and he wanted to hang out so I tell him to meet me at the Marshmallow Hut in 2 hours. He said fine.

"Charlie texted me back he said that the picture is at least 40 years old and there's other imprints on the photo."

"Okay, that's something that needs to be checked out. Tell him that you will be there in 2 hours. You will take my car and head back to the dorm, while I have dessert with Benny Hampton."

"Go Girl, he is a looker."

"Yes, he seems to be true right now, but I'm single so I will have this little dessert with him." "Now back to work"

"We laugh and get back to the books"

"I am sitting there going through the first book, of Hawkins when Rebecca Chasten walks up"

Rebecca Chasten:

"Well, well what are you guys up to?"

"What do you want Chasten?"

"I just saw you guys driving over here so I dropped by to see what the latest was?

"Well there is nothing for you, here or with us."

"See that is where you are wrong Carmen, I just had a little visit probably wasn't even 10 minutes long with your dear friend Megan and she gave me something that I think you might want."

"I don't want what you're selling Chasten; now please leave me to what I am doing."

I knew Megan was up to something, now the only thing is why and why would she trust Rebecca?

"Wrong again Carmen, for you to be the junior journalist you is sure wrong a lot."

"Chasten either tell me why you're here or vamoose."

"There is nothing to tell, just only came to give you these back. You're missing them right?"

On the table she threw the missing pages out of Ms. Jameson's journal.

"How did you get these?"

"How else, Megan Parex Oh wait a minute, you really think I'm making this up. Well suppose I can't blame you for that, but seriously I am not out for you, I am out for no one, but if I did have to pick who... it would be Megan, for my own personal reasons it would be her. This here is merely a token to show you even your friends can be just as crooked as me. Goodbye Ladies, hope that helps, with the Stacy Dugal story, and oh, loved the article today!"

She turns around and walks off. I grabbed the pages and yep, it was from the journal. Why would Megan do this? I stop looking through the books to flip through these pages...

They seemed to be everywhere, but one thing was for sure Ms. Jameson went through a lot of emotions with Patrick Ferris...Journal [10 pages]...

Beverly Jamison,

We spent the day together and I loved every moment of it. I don't kno what to do now that I know why he truly brought me out here to Penelope Bridge... Pg-44

He had Lexington send me a note telling me that he wanted to see me the end of the day at the track field. I couldn't wait to get out of class. I just kne that he was going to give me his pin or ask me to marry him... Pg-24

Today in dance I overheard Kara Moberly telling Lindsey Middleton th MGP was giving his pin to a special girl. I couldn't believe it... Pg-18

Today is the last day I will ever speak to MICHAEL GREGORY PAREX, he hu me so bad. How do you tell someone you love them over and over, but then take away like it never happened? Daddy was right I needed to marry Patrick Ferris, i was going to be truly happy...Pg-56

MGP MGP MGP MGP MGP MGP MGP MGP MGP MGP MGP MGP MG MGP MGP MGP MGP MGP MGP MGP MGP MGP MGP MGP MGP MGP MGP MG MGP MGP MGP MGP MGP MGP ...Pg-58

Today I was asked to the Devils Dance by Patrick Ferris, but I am sick s mom said I couldn't go. Shucks! Pg-62

This morning I found out that Patrick Ferris was killed at the Devils Dance la night! I am so shocked and hurt. I should've been with him. My mom was ramblin to me about the Hawkins curse she tells me that's why she didn't let me go. cannot believe this. Who do I tell, what do I do? Pg-65

Out of all the pages I was only able to read 7, the rest of the pages were too old and the writing smudged off. But on all the pages the dates were blocked out, like Ms. Jameson had just enough time to take care of that before being wacked in the head by Celine. Well one thing's for sure, Michael Gregory is a Parex and Megan had to have known this before today, that's why she was at the hospital and that's why she ripped these pages out.

The million dollar question was why. Why would she rip them out, what does Michael Gregory Parex have to do with any of this? I look at my watch and I have about 45 minutes until I meet up with Benny Hampton. I get back into the books.

Peninsky: "Carmen I found something here about Charles Hawkins"
"Let me see"

Reading the Book it say's: Charles Hawkins, Owner of the Oil industry here in Medico, and the Sugar, water and cotton Mill. One day the wife Penelope came home to find that Charles had just simply vanished. She had no idea where he went. Calling the authorities they checked all over Medico, but never found him, when Penelope was on her death bed she said "Charles is not dead, he is punishing me...I know it. What one man does will forever cast a dark light over any that has gained from this one man's wrong doing? You cannot run from this. Just because your eyes are open, doesn't mean you are seeing the truth in front of you, even the plainest things can be kept from sight, your job is to separate the plainest things and the lies that are keeping you from seeing what's in front of you. Then she died, it was never confirmed if she had yellow fever or not. The doctors just knew that she was terminally ill and there was nothing they could do to help her.

"I stop reading and it hit me Ms. Lexington said that to me. There was a reason she said this to me."

"Okay Peninsky go ahead and take my car, if I get done early I will call or text you or I might have Benny bring me back. Just don't trust anyone or speak of this. Okay?"

"Yes, of course. What do you want to do with all these books, let's put them back we don't need anyone figuring out what we were up to in here calling this a small town was an understatement."

"I and Peninsky put each of the books back, he took my car and I took all the notes and put them in the trunk."

"Don't forget to lock the car doors and make sure you do not go in the trunk. It's too much stuff for me to take with me on this dessert date. Be careful, do what you need to do because tonight you're staying with me right?"

"Yes, we have a lot of stuff to make a connective gram for."

"Okay, Outcha!"

"Outcha!"

We leave off in different directions and I began walking down the road and around the corner, when I run into Rebecca Chasten

Rebecca Chasten Part 2:

"So, were you able to use those pages?"
"If you're looking for a thank you Rebecca you won't get it from me"
"No I am not looking for any appreciation, I am just wondering if I helped you in anyway?"
"I am not telling you anything Rebecca, and can you stop following me."
"I just want to talk, no games no nothing. I know something that you don't and you kind of look like you have been traveling in circles so I just want to help."
"What Rebecca? What do we possibly have to talk about?"

While Rebecca was cutting me off from my dessert date I received a text from Benny saying "Hey I'm waiting on you beautiful."
I immediately started to smile and text him back telling him I was just a few minutes away.
"So what do we have to talk about?"
"Why Megan Parex tried to hide those pages... "
"Why did she try to hide the pages Rebecca?"
"Because she is an Air to the Hawkins family, her whole family is."
"What? Do you even know what you are talking about?"
"I'm going to leave you at that, you know where to find me when you're ready to get me on record".
She twirled off and smirked like she had a major ball to drop and I was net-less. I turned back into the direction of the Marshmallow Hut and was anxious to eat and see Benny. When I arrived I could see him through the window, looking so fine and so manly. I needed to say a quick prayer it's been a while since I have had male, real male company or did a sneak out one night just to be a little naughty. *"Jesus, please let tonight be the best experience—okay one of the best experiences of my lifetime. Let me intrigue this man to where he will keep coming back and he will continue wanting to know Carmen Maronii. Please O, lord let him see pass my flaws and still like me to where he can eventually love me, flaws and all. Amen."*

I walk in the restaurant and pull up a chair

Meeting Benny Hampton: Chapter 12

"Hello, Mr. Hampton you clean up really well"

"What? You didn't think I looked good, in my orderly uniform?"

"Ha, Ha, Ha you looked great Benny."

"We locked eyes again like we once did at Medico Asylum"

"I-I-I didn't think you knew where the Marshmallow Hut was."

"Of course what is it, because I'm black? Ha, ha I'm just kidding"

"I know you were, because I am Black, Italian and white so I know it has nothing to do with race."

"Okay, I like a feisty woman. So beautiful Miss Carmen what would you like to order."

"I grab a menu and begin to find me a large banana split with creamed marshmallow sauce"

"You're not going to look at a menu, or have you already ordered..."

We laugh

"No, I would never order without you."

You would have thought we have been together for years, but nope we just met and he already was flattering me and pulling me in

"Well I have to tell you something Miss Carmen"

"I began to look up at the sky and tell Jesus I know you tried, but I guess he just wasn't for me.

"What is that?"

"Well, this is my father right here. Joe Hampton"

"Nice to meet you Mr. Hampton I am---"

Joe: "You don't have to tell me my son has already told me all about the young beautiful lady who swept him off his feet. Nice to meet you Miss Carmen"

"I smile and I look back at him and say..."

"Oh, yeah! So Mr. Hampton if you don't mind me why is you here?"

Benny: "Well see that's what I wanted to tell you, my dad owns Marshmallow Hut.'

"What? Are you kidding me...?"

"No not kidding, so that is how I knew where Marshmallow Hut was, I have been his biggest customer "[he chuckles and his dad pats him on the back]

Joe: "Miss Carmen"

"Yes sir."

Joe: "What will you have today?"

"First class service I like this."

We all laugh and I tell him...

"Twin towers Banana Bang Split with extra Marshmallow sauce hold the cherries... "

"He walks away with my order, and Benny looks back at me and say's..."

"So you're fine with this?"
"Yes, of course why would you think I wouldn't be?"
"I just didn't want you to think I was some rich arrogant guy"
"Well, now I don't think that I think you are one of the best guys I have ever met."

Sitting there with Benny, it made me feel alive and free; I was able to feel like a million bucks with just this simple man. I loved it, every minute of it. I look out the window and to my shock I see Jake Becham. He stares at me I didn't give him the satisfaction of seeing me look, so I turned back around to Benny who was all into me. We get our sundaes and have a lovely conversation. He tells me about his work at the Asylum and since he last had a date. I tell him about my work at Hawkins and that I am not originally from Medico. We sat there and talked for hours until I got a text on my phone from Peninsky...

Text:

"Found a lot in this photo, let me know when you're headed back I will be at your dorm room."

Text Ended!!!

I forgot all about the story, and that I was supposed to be meeting Peninsky.

"Benny can you take me back to campus"
"Yeah, sure anything for you"

I smiled and just fell head over heels
"Can I ask you something Carmen?"
"Shoot! "
"I like you, I mean really like you and I know this is our first date, but I would like to have another and hopefully something will come out of this one and many more."
"I am fine with that Benny; I would love to have another date with you"

He leaned over and kissed me and I just kissed him back, in the stage I was in I could have licked the ice cream off his fingers but I kept my tongue in my mouth. But the kiss I let him do what he wanted with those lips to my lips. He leaned back over and said...

"You have soft lips, I like"

"Thank you, you do to."

"Is it safe to say this will go far?"

"Yes it is Benny, yes it is"

We packed up, he said goodbye to his dad and walked me out and to his car.

Driving to the dorm I text Peninsky to let him know I am on my way. I couldn't help, but to notice that Benny was staring at me.

"I see you"

"See what? [He laughs]

"Okay, you got me. I love looking at you I just feel good when I am around you."

"I understand that feeling; I wish that we could spend a little more time together."

"That's okay I will definitely text you and if you got time in the morning can we meet for breakfast at Coffee Central maybe get a Danish."

[I laugh]

"Yes that would be great, you want me to meet you there or would you prefer to come pick me up?"

"I most certainly will come pick you up, that means I get some extra me time."

"Oh really, me time huh?"

"Yes, me and you."

We both flirt with each other I make my way towards his hands I just lock fingers with him. I know we just met, but when it feels right it feels right.

He locks fingers with me and kisses my hand, then winks at me. Gosh this man is making crazy.

"So what you doing tonight Mr. Hampton"

"You really like calling me that. [Ha, ha, ha] Well I am going to head back to the Hut and help dad, for a bit then head home. Did you want me to come back or did you need something. "Whatever you want beautiful?"

"No, no you are fine. I just wanted to make sure that I wasn't imposing on anything."

"You couldn't possibly do that, what do you have planned for the night Ms. Journalist"

"I am going to look over some notes and discuss them with my partner on this article then we will head to bed. And I will see you at 9am sharp. Deal"

"Okay, that is a definite deal, pinky promise."

We laugh out loud and by then we were pulling in through the gates of Hawkins School for Girls.

I show him where to drive to, we pull up he comes and opens my door. We share a couple of goodnight words and then I kiss him again.

"Goodnight Carmen, wait you never told me your last name"

"It's Carmen Maronii"

"Maronii, I like it. You have a good night and I will be back here at 9am sharp."

"Night!"

We smile at each other and he drives off.

There on to us: Chapter: 13

"I began walking up to the room, when Peninsky runs up behind me"

"I just texted you, you get it"

"What?"

"I was just telling you I was running around here"

"Oh, okay"

"So how was the gorgeous Hampton?"

"He was awesome. I loved every minute of it he was such a gentlemen, I think me and him might actually have something here"

"That is great. Be happy!"

We walk up to my floor, heading down to my room. Peninsky says...

"Why does it look like your door is open?"

"That's a good question"

"We take off down the hall. Come to my room and it is trashed."

"Peninsky have you came in here at all today.'

"Nope once I left you I went straight to Charlie and then my dorm to clean up and pack my stuff"

"Whoever did this is "On to us" they came in here looking for something. Are the papers and everything still in the trunk of the car?"

"Last time I checked"

We began heading to the student parking, we run to my car and pop open the trunk, a sigh of relief came upon us. Everything was like I left it. I and Peninsky immediately start thinking of people who could have done this. We had Rebecca, Megan, Lisa and wherever Tammy was as well as anyone who knew we went to see Ms. Elaine Ferris. It was getting real unsafe. I think it was time to go visit Celine Norman in jail. The first thing that we did was, go back to the Dorm and clean up the mess left behind after someone trashed my room.

Cleaning up I came across a note... "DORM J, ROOM JG/12, Maronii, Little Flower Face on Door; FIND THAT RING AND PAPERS" Well what do you know; someone had instructions on how to find me and what to look for once at my dorm room. Dummies must have not been too smart because they left evidence leading to whoever might be behind this. This game I was playing, because it was a game a really upside down one and I was so far in. I couldn't help but to think of Ms. Lexington the last time I seen her, before her death when she said".

"You can have all the pieces and still be way behind the game, when it comes to using the pieces handed to you. Don't pay so much attention to the fact that your winning, focus on the little things, listen, observe and be precise. A loser can sometime be a winner depending on how they play the game." I think I was getting closer to understanding that. Peninsky and me clean up the mess and I show him the paper left behind by whomever, he points out to me that he has seen this hand writing before he just can't remember just where he seen it.

We check the whole room to see if there is anything else, but it was clear. I look at my phone for the time, it was 11pm, I'm trying to figure out where the hell the time went, but when I relive the day in my head it becomes very clear where the time went. I text Benny to make sure he got home safe "Hey, just wanted to make sure you got home safe. Did you?" Peninsky begins to tell me all about what him and Charlie Discovered...

Charlie and Peninsky Ms. Jameson Photo Discovery:

"Okay, so after I left you, I met with Charlie had him take a look at the picture he immediately knew it was from March 1960, also I did a little more research on the Hawkins family it led me to Hawkins actual children a couple have died and that's it on them. Others either got married or just left the family."

"Really"

"Yeah, But the photo...Charlie looked on the back and noticed there was a watermark. So he scanned the picture to his computer and noticed..."

"What?"

"Who all do you see in this picture?"

"Ms. Jameson, Ms. Lexington, I don't know who this is, [he interrupts me to say... that's my great, great, great granddaddy Lewis Peninsky], Robert Ferris, *Elaine George*, and Hilary Norman, Michael Parex. So Ms. Elaine's maiden name was George. There is a watermark that says "Medico, Print 1912"...Hmm so what about the picture?"

"Look here on the back in the imprint now normally considering the years on this photo and how it was kept, you wouldn't be able to see this in normal light with normal eyes, but if you look closely. There is a signature..."

"I see, does that say Chasten?"

"Yes, it sure does"

"E. Chasten"

"So is she the one taking the picture?"

'I am assuming, because she is not in it."

"Okay, well the first thing is to find out who E. Chasten is and why she was here during the 60's at Hawkins"

It started to make sense why Rebecca wanted to help so much, her family was also a part of this mystery. But how did the Chastens fall into this. We began to go through some of the notes that we collected yesterday, but nothing had any relativity to any Chastens. We needed to get back to the Library and look through those books again, or I could just ask Rebecca, but how? I didn't need her knowing that I knew she was connected to this as well.

Okay, Peninsky we need to make a connective gram for everything that we have right now, before we add anything else.

Your right, because we already have load of information now

I receive a text from Benny and he tells me that he was just helping his dad close up and that he misses me. I miss him to be honest, but I couldn't rush this with him. I texted him back letting him know that I did, and I couldn't wait to see him in the morning.

Me and Peninsky Connective Gram:

Stacy Dugal
Celine Norman
Roomy with Stacy Dugal
In Jail
Related to Hilary Norman
Lisa Fredricks
Grandmother Danity Fredrick's/Ferris
Descendant of Hawkins G-G-G grandson Robert
Help dispose of Stacy Dugals Bed sheets
Sent Melody to trash and break in my room
Wanted to Kill Tammy Dugal
Had motive to kill Ms.
Tammy Dugal
Sister of Stacy Dugal
She has disappeared?
Melody Hampton
Helped Dispose of Stacy Dugals Bed
Roommates with Tammy
Sister of Benny Hampton [Orderly at M.I.A]
Left a journal behind, a ring with the initials MGP and 3 bank statements.
Hawkins School for Girl
Ms. Beverly Jameson
KILLED by Celine Norman??
Ms. Gina Lexington
Ms. Martha Peters
Class of 1960
Gina Lexington
Beverly Jameson
Michael Parex
Hilary Norman
Lewis Peninsky
Elaine George
? Chasten
This person took the "Class of 1960 photo?"
Suspects
Rebecca Chasten
Megan Parex
Descendant of Michael Parex
Ripped pages out of Ms. Jameson's journal
Tammy Dugal
Melody Hampton
Broke into my room
Sent Lisa to break into my room, but
Lisa Fredrick's
Could have possibly killed
Possibly framed Celine Norman for the murder of Ms. Jameson
Working for or with Megan Parex
Celine Norman
Main perosn in Disposing of Stacy
Martha Peters
Died 1940
Charles/Penelope Hawkins
Henry Hawkins
Charles/Penelope Hawkins
Macy Hawkins
Married a Southern Banker from Texas last name Bellon
Rachel Hawkins
Never Heard from
George Hawkins
Married Debbie Cleveland from Montegomery, Alabama.
Charles Hawkins Jr.
Died in Plane Crash
Brad Hawkins
In Denver
In an Retirement

So here we have the official Connective gram of everything we have so far. Me and Peninsky just stand back and look at all the papers and sticky tabs and markers and names and we notice that all these people have two things in common. HAWKINS SCHOOL AND THE HAWKINS NAME, Peninsky grabs the photo and places it dead in the center of the Gram while looking at it; it looked like we had figured this all out. We left the Gram on the floor and began getting ready for what was going to come of tomorrow....

We have to begin getting ready for the Masquerade Ball at some point tomorrow. I am still trying to figure out all of this though who knows what will come out of today, we might just get lucky and wrap this up before noon.

I chuckle sarcastically because we just now got some of the biggest pieces from Ms. Elaine Ferris and I still needed to find Robert Ferris's father and Marguerite Fredrick's. There was still so much to do and I think the Masquerade Ball was going to be the worst of it all. I received a text from Benny asking me to meet him outside...

Meeting Melody Hampton:

"What's up Mr. Hampton?"

"I need to talk to you, Carmen"

"Okay, what's wrong you look like you have been running a marathon?"

"Benny looked nervous shaken up and like he had ran a marathon cross country"

"It's about that Dugal girl"

What did Benny have to do with this? Please don't tell me that I am going to have to end up ending all ties with him.

"Remember when I told you that my sister goes here?"

"Yes, I remember what about her?"

"She lives on Midas, Rowe..."

'I began to figure out what was going on here..."

"What does she know, Benny?"

"She knows what happened to Tammy Dugal..."

"I knew Celine said that I would never find Tammy Dugal, but I didn't think she was serious."

"What about Tammy Dugal? Can you come up to my room with me?"

"I need you to meet someone first"

Benny opens up the door to his truck and there she was.

"I know her"

"Benny slammed his truck door"

"What, I thought you said you didn't know my sister Carmen?"

"Well I don't know her, I just only met her today and it was for like 10 seconds"

"I put my hand on his chest and told him that all would be okay, he can trust me. He opened his truck door back up."

"Hello, Melody I am Carmen, but you can call me Maronii if you like."

She looked fragile and like she has been crying for a while.

Benny: "Melody its okay, we're going to go up to her room and talk about this."

"Melody if you don't want to talk to me that is fine, you can talk to your brother and he can talk to me and I can take notes and get what happened to Tammy Dugal."

She looked at me, and then said...

Melody: "It is okay, I will talk to you"

I was so happy that she wanted to talk to me. We got her out the car and up to my room, Peninsky was waiting anxiously, but I don't think he had any idea on what was coming next.

"Peninsky: What's going on Maronii?"

"This is Melody and you already know Mr. Hampton"

"Peninsky: Yes, Hey Mr. Hampton"

They both spoke and we got Melody in the room and shut and locked the door, closed the curtain and sat her down.

"Okay, Melody this is my best friend Peninsky, he will be in here as well you can trust him."

"She looked at me and then at Peninsky..."

"Melody: He's fine. Are you-u- hmm Gay?"

We all stopped and looked at each other, and then Peninsky said...

Peninsky: "Well yes, girl"

Then he laughed, so we all laughed. It seemed to put Melody in a comfort place..

"Is it okay if I get this on the record? "

"Yes that is fine"

"So melody where is Tammy Dugal?"

We set back and listened; I got my pad out and began to take notes.

Melody Hampton's Story...

"Well first I have to let you know I am Tammy Dugal's roommate.

Well I kind of seen that coming
"Okay!"

"It was Thursday night I was in the GYM that night, practicing for the Volleyball playoffs Saturday. When Celine and Lisa came into the GYM screaming at each other, Lisa was saying how Tammy was the weak link that she needed to be taken care of. Celine was trying to convince Lisa that Tammy was not the problem that Carmen Maronii was..."

It didn't shock me that they were talking about me, but hinting at a direction of taking care of me was shocking.

"I have a question or two for you Melody"

"Okay?"

"You said that you were in the "GYM" did they see you?"

"No, if they did they kept talking anyway"

"Okay and my other question was has Tammy Dugal ever mentioned anything about her sister Stacy Dugal since her disappearance?"

"That night, Stacy disappeared she didn't come out her room, I tried to tell her it was about her sister that she should come talk with the police, but honestly Carmen I think she already knew she was missing"

"Why do you think that Melody?"

"Because she was huddled up in the middle of her bed rocking and holding her knees, on the floor she pulled out some of her hair. Now Tammy Pulling out her hair was not normal. Normal for her is lying in her bed for hours before and after classes repeating "The Hawk carried a sword that struck the Ferry who left the sorrows to a Bellon, that needed help from the Dugal" She would repeat that over and over. I just assumed she was praying in a different language, but I don't know."

She was repeating the names of the descendants this was starting to link more and more

"Are you sure Melody it was in that order?"

"Yes, it was a catchy little rhyme or whatever it was."

"Okay, continue Melody"

"I underlined that rhyme"

Benny: "is any of this making any sense to you, Carmen?"

Well, unfortunately yes, Benny and now your sister and you are a part of this. I'm sorry.

Benny, looked overwhelm but he stayed by his sisters side. Melody continued her story.

"Lisa sounded angrier when Celine didn't agree with her. Then Tammy came into the GYM, looking for me when she came upon Lisa and Celine. She just froze then Lisa walked over to her and asked her what she was doing in the GYM so late. Tammy told her that she was looking for me to ask about the Masquerade Ball. Lisa put her hands on Tammy shoulder and then began to walk her out...

"Melody where was Celine?"

She was pacing back and forth talking to herself"

"So Celine really didn't want to participate?"

"From the looks no she didn't"

"You can continue..."

"Tammy turned around and she seen Celine pacing looking worried, she asked Lisa what was wrong? Lisa told her to wait outside while she talks with Celine. Tammy went outside; Lisa walked over to Celine and told her to get herself together. Celine started raving about "The Norman Family" something about how in 1970 something. Celine told Lisa that they needed to focus on you, because you were the one working on the Stacy Dugal story. Lisa kept telling Celine that, they would work on you after Tammy. Celine told Lisa that they should send Tammy to your dorm room to see what all you knew. Lisa agreed... They told Tammy to come back in; they began to tell her what to do when she started to panic. She began running and that's when Lisa ran after her and Celine followed. After that I don't know what happened...

"Okay so, Melody did you see Tammy anymore?"

"Nope, when I came to the Dorm Lisa approached me..."

[Melody had a pause, and she began to fidget. That's when Benny grabbed her hands and told her to tell me.]

"What's wrong Melody?"

"Lisa approached me and asked me if I would do her a favor?"

"Okay, what was the favor?"

"She handed me a piece of paper and told me to not open it until I was out of the dorm. "When I got out of the dorm then I was to read the paper. I initially told her no I don't want to have anything more to do with her or Celine."

"What do you mean anything more? Were you all friends?"

"No, WE WERE NOT! They used me like they used Tammy and Stacy. "

"So what went on next Melody?"

"When I turned around to walk up the steps she grabbed my pony tail and pulled me to the back corner of the hallway. She threatened to tell everyone that she caught me and Stacy kissing in the girl's showers. "

I was not expecting that, Melody began to cry and say she was sorry.

It's okay, Melody I am not here to judge only to find the truth. Was that all she said to you?

"No, she threatened to tell the police that I got rid of Stacy's sheets off her bed."

"Why would she do that? What happened?"

Wednesday night I was sleep in my room, when Celine and Lisa came and woke me and Tammy up. We went with them back to Celine's room. Celine began to take all of Stacy's sheets off of her bed and told me and Tammy to put them in the plastic wrapping that Lisa had and bury them in the Forbidden Trees. I and Tammy said no, but then Celine told us we were now a part of this and we had no choice. Tammy started to ask where her sister was. Celine told her she didn't know but if we all didn't want to go to jail we had to do this, because the police were on their way. We took the bag Celine told us that Lisa would go with us and she would stay back to make sure that everything went okay when the police arrived, because she was the roommate it would look weird if she left. She said she would meet us in the Forest after the cops left for us to just wait there.

"So that's why she was threatening you? You and Tammy were the only two who knew what she and Celine had done."

So after she pushed me on the wall she told me again exactly what to do and do it now. So I grabbed the piece of paper and left the dorm. When I got outside I opened the paper and it read... "DORM J, ROOM JG/12, Maronii, Little Flower Face on Door; FIND THAT RING AND PAPERS"I had no clue that it was your room, swear it. I headed to the dorm when I came to the room, I knew it was locked so I ran into a student she just so happened to be an assistant to the head of household she was in such a rush I told her that I was locked out of my room, she reached in her pockets and unlocked the door, and told me not to do it again. I went through the room looking for the items on the paper, but I came across nothing, not even you. I went back to my dorm Lisa was waiting for me in my room, I told her I couldn't find anything she became furious she began raving how someone named Parex was going to be furious and that Maronii needs to leave things alone, that she would be dealt with soon. She noticed I still was there and she left and told me not to say anything and left. Right after she left I went home. That's when my brother came and he was telling me how he "had a date with the girl Carmen the journalist from my school, he began telling me that you guys were going to go on a coffee date in the morning I could tell he really was interested in you so I told him everything."

-End of Melodies Story!-

"He told me that we had to tell you, because you were the only one that could help me. That's it, I swear!"

Peninsky fell back in his seat, blew a breath and looked at me to see what I was going to do. Thinking, this girl ran sacked my room, broke into it illegally and she had some dealings with the disappearance of Stacy Dugal and she could know more than what she was letting on. But I honestly wasn't shocked. I really became more infatuated and into her brother because she would have never came to me with this hadn't he not told her and trusted me. He really was a good guy.

"Okay, Melody thanks for opening up, but I have to ask you something. This will tell me if I can trust you or not. Okay"

"Yes, I understand, but I just told you everything"

"I know and I heard everything you said, but I need to know... Are you positive that you did not know that this was my room?"

"She looked at her brother and at Peninsky she begun fidgeting again. Benny told her to tell me."

"No, I didn't I really didn't"

I looked at Peninsky; he smirked and then shook his head. Benny looked at me hoping that this didn't kill our beginning friendship. I looked at him and smiled; because I didn't think wrong of him I just now knew that I couldn't trust his sister. Shoot she could be working for Lisa right now.

"Okay, great! Okay one more question. Do you know what happened with Celine and Ms. Jameson?"

"She didn't hesitate at all."

"So I kind of figured her out, when she was lying she would fidget and when she wasn't she was calm."

"Yes I know what happened, well not the actual incident I just know I heard Celine and Ms. Jameson having an argument."

"Okay, tell me what you do know"

"She started to tell us..."

"Well that morning it had to be 5:00 in the morning I was up getting ready for practice in the gym with some of my teammates, when I heard Lisa yelling at Celine in the laundry room..."

"What did she say?"

"She was telling Celine that if she knew Ms. Jameson had visited you, that now Ms. Jameson was a problem as well. Celine was telling Lisa that you can't just going around getting rid of people that you don't like and definitely not teachers. So Lisa told Celine she could do what she wanted, but Celine had until after Lisa came back from her run to handle this with Ms. Jameson. Celine told Lisa that she would talk to her; Ms. Jameson wouldn't say anything that she was okay. Lisa told Celine she didn't care and that Ms. Jameson had to go now or later. Lisa began walking out of the laundry room, so I had to take off. That was all I heard. It wasn't until I came back from practice that I saw the officers and Ms. Jameson on the stretcher and Celine in handcuffs I guess she took care of Ms. Jameson now rather than later."

Well that lines things up with that mystery, now all I had to do was get Celine's story and if it matched up with Melody's, Melody might've actually earned a few cool points back from me.

"Thanks for sharing Melody I will definitely be in touch with you, okay"

"Okay, thanks for listening and I am sorry that I trashed your room. I really am"

"Oh, don't worry about it I could hear Peninsky gasp, like what you mean? Don't worry about it, we had to clean that mess up girl."

Benny began to walk Melody out the door and told her to wait on him in the car. He asked me could I walk him out. I insisted

Benny grabbed my hand and we walked out together and he thanked me for listening and trusting him. I thanked him for trusting me, but I needed to tell him something that he may want to know... He just stopped and looked me dead in my eyes and said "What's wrong Beautiful?"

"Benny I don't know how to tell you this, but your sister was lying when she said that she didn't know that it was my room she broke into. I am only telling you so you can make the choice on the things she said whether she was telling the truth or not. I know that you can't choose sides but I would never make you, I just know that I am into this story and I am not finishing until I have made all the lies present and the liars have surface and the truth can be seen in the light. That's what a good and loyal journalist does and there is too much that has happened for me not to finish what I have started and now that I know your sister is a part of this I am not going to the authorities, but everyone will be held accountable for his/her actions no matter the role by time all this surface. I'm sorry!"

He looked at me and said...

"I know Carmen and I understand and I would never, expect anything less of you. I still want us to be something what I don't know, but I don't want to be without you. Do you understand?"

"Yes, I do...What about your sister

We both take a look at the car and we look at Melody and then he looks at me.

"She is a big girl and the first thing my father taught us was "just because the sun isn't shining right now, doesn't mean it will never shine again. Just means we have some rains to help wash away mistake stains. We'll get through anything that comes out of this and I will be by her side, but I won't lie or manipulate for her."

We both smiled and he kissed me and I loved every minute of it, he told me goodnight and I said I will see you in the morning 9am Mr. Hampton

He got in the truck blew me a kiss and drove off. Heading back upstairs I couldn't help, but to think Lisa was calling all of the shots and Celine was merely a puppet, I think she really thought that her and Lisa were friends, but Lisa seen that anyone who knew of what she had done needed to go including the one person who helped her do it.

Reaching the room, Peninsky was already asleep. I knew he was tired, but dang. After seeing him sleep it didn't take me to long to fall behind. But something played on my mind like a song... Melody said "Parex was going to be furious", I think Megan sent Lisa to come to my room, but Lisa couldn't do it so she got Melody. I knew Megan was trying something, can't trust anyone. Before I could go to sleep, something jumped in my mind. I see Celine heading out into the Forest the night Stacy Dugal was officially missing and she was reaching for something in her back pocket. Could Stacy and Tammy Dugal be in the forest? I needed to find out, but I couldn't do it now, it was too late. Or could I? I woke up Peninsky and told him we have to take a walk in the Forest. The look upon his face was enough to scare anyone. I texted Benny and asked him if he could come back with a Flash light and a shovel. He immediately texted me back and said he was on his way. I told him me and Peninsky would meet him out front.

"Peninsky we must go into the forest, I think the Dugal girls are out there."

"Maronii, you cannot be serious..."

"Yes I am and Benny, is on his way back I may just let him stay the night considering he's doing all of this back and forth and we do have a breakfast date at 9 which is in 8 hours."

I couldn't believe it, it was already 1 in the morning this case was taking a hold of me and the day ahead was going to be a wreck. Peninsky and I get ourselves together I grab my pad and pen and he grabs my video camera; we head outside to meet Benny...

Forbidden Trees: Chapter 14
"I, Peninsky and Benny Hampton Investigate Part 1"

Meeting up with Benny outside seemed like a dream come true, even though I just seen him, He hugged me and handed me the flash lights and he carried the shovel.

"What's this all for Carmen"

"I'm scared if I tell you might run." [He laughs]

"I'm not leaving my woman- I-I-I mean I wouldn't leave you out here alone you or Peninsky"

Peninsky nudges me with his elbow and smiles; I smile back and lean into Benny...

"Your woman huh"

"Well you know, that's what I am working on with you right..."

I smile and say definitely, I like that. He kisses me and says...

"So you going to tell me why I brought you a shovel and some flash lights at 1 in the morning"

"Well when you left, it hit me that I saw Celine the night Stacy Dugal disappeared and she was running into the Forest, it didn't hit me with a reason why she was, until Melody said that she told them to go out there and wait on her."

"Okay, that's right nice catch beautiful"

"Thank you Mr. Hampton"

We flirted and I just couldn't keep him out my mind or eyes, and he felt the same way. It's crazy because I know we just met, but he was real no book, no movie no vivid imagination of mine and if he was interested why wouldn't I show him I am too. I don't plan on playing games with Benny and I can tell he doesn't either

"So where is Melody now?"

"She's at home with my mom and dad"

"Was she okay, once she left?"

"Yeah, about as okay as she ever would be considering all she has seen and heard and done"

We all walked down the road until we came across the path that leads you into the forest. Peninsky was surfing on his phone and listening to music while I and Benny held our own conversation.

"So, what you think you're going to find out here"

"I am hoping 3 things… We find the sheets they brought out here, Lisa Fredrick's out here trying to cover up all that has happened and Tammy or Stacy Dugal. All I know there is something out here and we all just have to go look"

"Okay, I will help no problem just as long as we make our breakfast date

We both laughed and then I asked him…

"Yes, I am glad you mentioned that.

He stopped so I stopped we were both facing each other, he grabbed me by my hand and said what's up?

"I wanted to know if you wanted to stay the night, because I know you have been back and forth, and I didn't want you to have to drive--- [he cut me off and kissed me so softly and said…]

"Of course I will do anything for you. I can't wait to hold you and definitely see how you are with Coffee in your system."

I just stood there smiling and just feeling lovely. FOR THE FIRST TIME IN MY LIFE I FEEL LIKE I HAVE SOMETHING REAL.

I turn around and Peninsky was looking at us smiling we all laughed and entered the woods.

Forbidden Tree Number 4-260:

We walked and walked for hours. We were just going to give up when Benny heard a noise coming from the right of us. At Hawkins the Forbidden Forest use to be a Garden that Penelope or someone in the family started to grow fresh produce for lunch here and other things, well it was divided into sections of numbers the 4 meaning Hawkins and the dash signifying that there was a new section beginning I believed. Well after the garden died I guess whoever changed the name and planted trees here never took away the numbering system.

We followed Benny; it was nice to have a strong man with us, because I and Peninsky were some girls. We came across Tree 4-260 we had no clue what we were walking into. Peninsky walked over to the tag that read 4-260.

"Maronii there is some weird symbol here…"

I followed behind when I fell into a pit. Peninsky and Benny immediately tried to help me; I stopped moving around and told them to hold on because something was down here…

"What you see Carmen?"

"I don't know yet... hand me a flashlight someone"

Peninsky: "girl is you okay?"

"Yeah just a little dirt, won't kill nobody"

"Benny hands me a flashlight. I turn it on..."

"Well I found, Stacy Dugal's bed sheets."

Peninsky/Benny: "Are you serious?"

"Yep and there is something else down here to..."

I began pulling the sheets back and I can't believe it...

"GET ME OUT OF HERE! NOW!!!"

I begin screaming at the top of my lungs; Benny picks me up with no problem.

We all look down in the pit...

Peninsky: "Is that a skull?"

"Yes, it is..."

Benny: "Whose is the question, it couldn't be Stacy or Tammy Dugal's this has been here longer than a day or two."

"Yeah, you're right Benny. Call 911 Peninsky."

"Yeah, right!"

Benny holds me and while we wait for the police

Medico, Police:

Who would have thought to come would be Detective Michaels and Sully.

"Hello, again Ms. Carmen"

"Hello, Detectives"

"So what we have here? Oh wow, so who have you killed now Carmen"

[He laughs sarcastically?]

"I have never killed anyone and this we stumbled upon, literally"

"Okay, let's say that's true, why were the 3 of you out here at 3:30 in the morning?"

"We wanted to show Benny the Forbidden Forest when we heard something and then just like that I fall into this grave I suppose and now you guys are here."

"Is this true Benny, what's your last name son? "

"Benny, Benny Hampton"

"Oh yeah I know your father he is your father right?"

"Yes sir, Joe Hampton"

"Okay and what's your name over here."

"Peninsky, Jacob"

The detective looked like he was startled when Peninsky said his name.

"Peninsky huh..?"

"Yes!"

"Okay you 3 can head back to your dorms and we will find you if we have more questions.

Wait a minute detective... we need to find out who this is"

"I understand Carmen, but your journalism stops at the gates at Hawkins. Do you understand? I will let you know what I can, is that fine?"

"I guess, but I believe that you will find a lot and you won't like what you do."

"Something already told me that once I seen you here"

He smirks at me and I smirk back, I think me and detective Sully is becoming okay with each other, that would be great because all that I have discovered I will need that trust within the police department.

We walk back to the dorm and get to the room; Peninsky took the couch and headed to sleep, I had to take a shower, and Benny cleaned himself up first and then waited at my desk for me to get out. I was overwhelmed, at everything that was happening around me, all surrounding one person it seemed to be like I was never going to get to the truth. I cleaned myself up then lay down with Benny looking at the clock I noticed that it read 4:45am we had less than 5 hours to get some sleep and be up for our breakfast date. Just sitting there all night he just looked at me and I looked back hoping he wouldn't want to stop being friends.

9am came very quick it didn't take us long to get ourselves together I left Peninsky to sleep and we headed on this date. In the car we couldn't help, but to talk about what we discovered early this morning in the Forbidden Tree's. Benny seemed more anxious to discuss it then me, but it was nice to have someone else finally seeing what I have been seeing the last couple of days. He started out asking me how I feel considering I was the one who fell in the grave of bones.

Honestly, I don't feel anything except trying to figure out whose head I maybe stepped on and how long it has been there?

"I can understand that... How do you think this is going to pan out with the police?"

"I am so glad you mentioned that, I am so sorry that you are caught up with this mess of a story with me."

"Why would you apologize for that Carmen?"

"I guess, because I asked you to come back and you ended up getting caught up in this mystery."

"Well, first Carmen you have to realize I chose to come back, no one made me"

"Okay, my second thing about the police is do you think that we could stop by there maybe Detective Sully has something new since we last seen him..."

"Yes, of course I was just thinking the same thing"

We drove into town first stop was Medico, Police Department.

Detective Sullies Investigation:

As soon as we walked into the station, I could see Detective Sully could see my face and expression from across the room.

Detective Sully: "Morning, Miss Carmen and Mr. Hampton"

Carmen/Benny: "Good Morning"

"So I suppose that you are visiting me to see what I have found"

"Of course, so what have you found?"

"Well follow me; remember when you told me I wasn't going to like what I see?"

"Yes, I am assuming with that statement and tone, you didn't?"

"No, I didn't but that is not my biggest worry"

"What do you mean?"

"How did you know? Once I done some investigating that I was not going to like what I found and furthermore how are you caught up in all of this?"

I was not expecting that, now my worry is how I am going to answer these serious questions? The good thing about right now is that he is actually more focused on showing me and Benny what he found. He leads us to the mortician.

Introducing Mortician Brenda Davenport:

"Carmen, Benny this is Brenda Davenport she is our head Mortician here. Miss Davenport can you tell them what you have found resulting from these bones"

Miss Davenport:

"Well to be short and frank the both of you have solved a puzzling mystery since the late 1900's."

"What is that Miss Davenport?"

"These bones are Charles Hawkins"

"Are you sure?"

"Well as sure as you and me having this discussion"

"How can this be?"

"Well, looking through some old records and files, when Mr. Charles Hawkins disappeared no one knew what happened to him, because there was no body, nor any sign of an abduction or anything so the town and I am assuming the Sheriff just made him a missing person, but more he just left the case at a dead end and never added anything more to it. Then from vital records and the skull and more this is a perfect match to Mr. Charles Hawkins."

"Well, that sort of explains a lot. Detective, couldn't you get in some type of trouble telling me and Benny this?"

"No not really, I am telling you because we would have never found this if you would have not found this so I am saying screw the rules on this one."

"Okay, fine so I have a question?"

"I am starting to find out Carmen that's all you ever have are questions"

I laugh and then flip open my pad, and ask him...

"Could you find out if Mrs. Penelope Hawkins actually died of Yellow Fever?"

He had this look like he was super confused

"Why would I look that up?"

"Well, this is her husband Mr. Sully and she told the doctors and police on her death bed that he was not dead. So that sounds like something to look into, don't you think?"

"Yes, it actually does but that is going to have to come from a family member"

Benny: "What do you mean?"

"Someone from the Hawkins family is going to have to approve the Exhumation of Penelope Hawkins"

"I know someone..."

[It immediately came to my mind Elaine Ferris]

"Who Carmen?"

"Elaine Ferris"

Detective Sully, turned around and placed his hand on his chest

"Okay, now why would I go ask a crazy woman who has been locked up for over 40 years in a patted room?"

"Because she is a Hawkins family member, crazy or not she is a relative and she can give the permission to exhume Penelope's Body correct?"

"Yes, you are. You are a smart girl"

Benny: "Yes she surely is"

He leans over to me grabs my hand, then kisses me.

"So Miss Carmen how are we going to get Elaine Ferris to give us the Okay to open up her Great Grandmothers grave"

"I'll just ask her"

"What? She is in Medico, Insane Asylum you can't just walk in there and say "hey I want to talk to Elaine Ferris and I am not a relative"

"Well, of course not, my best friend Benny Hampton is an orderly there so I am pretty sure he knows Ms. Elaine Ferris."

"Well that's all nice in theory, but we still have to run this by the right channels."

"Okay, you do that; I and Benny are late for a Breakfast Date. So excuse us. We'll be over at Coffee Central if you need us."

We walked off to head over to Coffee Central. Benny seemed like he was in a comfort zone. I found that a little weird so I asked him before we walked into Coffee Central....

"Benny, I have a question"

"Okay, what is it beautiful?"

"You have no affiliation with any of this mess do you?"

"WHY WOULD YOU THINK I WOULD?"

"You seemed like your relaxed and I am not saying that it is a bad thing I just have so much around me and the only person I have been able to trust that is still alive is Peninsky. So I have to ask?"

"Okay, I can understand that, but I am relaxed because I am with you for one, and then we are getting closer to some type of truth and that truth will help my sister. That is a wonderful reason to be relieved isn't it?"

"Yes, of course it is. I'm sorry I am just significantly paranoid, because the truth is coming out regardless of who hid it. I would hate to get close to you and you have been fooling me just to help yourself or sister."

"Never, remember I brought her to you and I didn't even know we would be talking or for that much be here. I had no clue my sister was going to be in this mess her first year of college. This is all new to me Carmen, please believe when I say that I am not playing any of these crazy games or playing you."

"I am so happy to hear that, and I believe you so let's get in here and enjoy our coffee and Danish"

We laughed and went in the store.

When going into Coffee Central I couldn't help, but to notice that the town seemed to know who I was and was really staring me and Benny down. Benny noticed it to, but he ignored it grabbed me by my hand and took me to a table.

"Benny, why do you think there staring?"

"Because they see this beautiful woman with me"

[Laughing sarcastically]

"I am serious"

"I think they are looking because it's probably starting to leak out about Hawkins"

"But how I have not spoken to anyone about what I have been finding"

"Well, Carmen the police did get called to Hawkins this morning, where there were bones in a pit, grave whatever that was."

"You're right."

We ordered our coffee talked some more about where this could go. Then the strangest thing happened...Peninsky stormed in.

"Carmen, Benny we have to go right now"

He looked startled and in a hurry.

"What's going on Peninsky?"

"Okay, well I was at the dorm you know looking over our connective Gram."

"Okay, what about it?"

"I have to show you..."

"Show me what?"

"Let's go to the library"

We headed over to the library... Peninsky was anxious and serious looking. He took us over to Book Shelf ML-H0290

"Why are we in the history section again? We checked all over here Peninsky"

"No! We thought we did, but when I looked at the connective gram it hit me that we didn't have anything on Penelope Hawkins or who she was before she was a Hawkins."

"Okay, we may not have anything on the connective gram yet, but that was just what we collected so far. We don't have anything on there about this morning either, doesn't mean it won't be"

"Just listen! Maronii"

"Listening"

Benny was just quiet he looked more interested than Peninsky.

He started to reach on the shelf, and then pulled out the Parex history book.

See I knew there was nothing here; we already looked in the Parex book

"MARONII"

"Okay, okay go ahead"

He flipped towards the end of the book and pulled out a wrinkled and old discolored paper it reads PH/Lane 1252H.

"What? PH/Lane 1252H"

I and Benny looked confused and still feeling like this had nothing to do with anything we were working on.

"That's why I came and got you two."

"So why and how is this relative to Penelope?"

"Because Maronii I asked the librarian what PH meant and she said "Penelope Hawkins"

"How did she know that?"

"She showed me all the memorials and statues that are around the town on this Map and anything that is a symbol of someone of importance like Penelope Hawkins it is marked with that person's initials."

"Are you serious?"

"Yep"

"So what of the Lane 1252H"

"The H stands for Hawkins so I am thinking the Penelope statue at Hawkins School for Girls"

"Wow, this is great Peninsky"

We all left the library and drove right over to the school.

[I received a phone call from Detective Sully]

☎ Phone Call:

"Hello"

DS: "Miss Carmen"

Hey, 'Mr. Sully"

DS: "Carmen could you meet me back at the police station in about an hour"

"Yes, what's wrong?"

DS: "Just need to discuss with you and your friends some of the other things I have found"

"Okay great we'll be there"

DS: "Okay"

PHONE CALL ENDED!!!!

Benny: "so did he find anything else?"

"Yeah, he wants us to meet him back at the station in an hour"

Benny/Peninsky: "that's cool"

"I was just thinking guys, tonight is the masquerade ball."

Peninsky: "yes, you are so right. I'm thinking we shouldn't go."

"Why you say that Peninsky"

"Because we have a lot to do today and because people die there"

"No one has died there in year's right?"

"I don't know"

"What you think Benny?"

"I know I want you to be safe, and if going is not going to secure that. Don't go!"

"Is your sister going? No, I put her on punishment for all that she has got herself into"

"Wow, okay, well if we're not going to go, we have to try to get the Dean to stop the Ball"

"How"

"Let's hope Detective Sully has found something good and this Lane 1252H will be a help"

We pull up to Hawkins, park and walk over to the administration office.

Envelope Hawkins: Chapter 15
"I, Peninsky and Benny Hampton Investigate Part 2"

Walking into the Administration office, we find the "Hawkins Directory"

"Hello, my name is..."

"Yes I know Carmen Maronii. I loved your piece in this season's issue"

"Thank you, we are doing another piece for the AAP and needed to find this Lane [Lane 1252H]"

"Okay, no problem do you have a signed viewers lease from your teacher or Senior Journalist?"

"No ma'am she just sent us over here before she had to leave out to get some things taken care of for the Masquerade Ball tonight. I'm sorry, but as soon as she gets back I will come right over with that lease."

"Okay, just this once Carmen, but note you have to have a viewer's lease for marked memorabilia in the school. These Lanes are private and historical and very old nothing should be touched or removed. Do you understand?"

"Yes ma'am we understand"

"Okay sign right here name, id numbers, and time and lane number"

We sign she hands us the lane number key that read "L1200" and tells us we have 30 minutes.

PH/Lane 1252H:

We unlocked the gate to the lane and begin looking for the lane sign reading "Lane 1252H" Splitting up. We noticed that anything that was old and a part of the Hawkins history was kept no matter how it looked or out of style it was. Some of these things were rusted falling apart and more. It looked as if they just built this building around the lanes and then fenced in all the old stuff.

"Peninsky: Over here"

I and Benny run over to Peninsky

"What is it?"

He just points up at the sign.

"Lane 1252H"

Sitting there was a wooden Box, but the box was sealed with an old lock, we were going to have a time trying to get this open.

Benny: "okay, well we need to find something to break this open"

"Yea, I know, but what? Everything out here would probably break soon as you touch it, it's so old"

"Peninsky let's just kick it"

"Okay, and then we're going to get in trouble for destruction of school property"

Benny: "Carmen we came out here to steal an item we don't know what, and lied to get back here to steal the item. I think we have crossed the line already for ethics and the law."

We chuckle and just like that Peninsky kicks the box and surprisingly the box fell apart all 4 corners just fell like ashes.

We moved around the ashes and lock and on the back of the lock it had that same strange symbol Peninsky mentioned in the forest."

Benny: "look"

Peninsky: "What is that?"

"It's a locket and a jewelry box"

We grabbed the locket and jewelry box and ran out of the lane. We headed back to my dorm room where Peninsky had the Connective Gram already out.

"Okay, so we need to open this jewelry box. What does the Locket say?"

Benny flipped it over.

Benny: "It says DMP Love Forever"

Peninsky and I stopped trying to open the jewelry box and walked over to Benny.

Peninsky: "I bet you that P means Parex"

"I don't doubt you on that Peninsky"

I open up the locket.

"And there it was... Penelope and this DMP"

Peninsky: "I have seen him before"

"Where"

"In that book"

"What book Peninsky?"

"T-T-T-The Parex history book"

We all just stopped Benny, looked like he had no clue what we were talking about.

We have to go back to the library, grab the connective gram

We rushed out where we were met by Rebecca Chasten and Megan Parex

Megan and Rebecca:

Megan: "Whoa! Stop, take a breath. Why are you running?"

Maronii: "Benny can you meet me and Peninsky at the car; we'll be there in just a second. Okay?"

Benny: "of course beautiful.

He kissed me then headed to the car.

Rebecca: "So Miss Maronii has a boyfriend? He is cute Carmen better watch out. Love Burns"

Maronii: "Don't mention anything about love considering I am still trying to figure out where your heart is. Whatever you have to say Rebecca choke on it, and then send me the bill because I will be happy to pay for your pain. Megan you looking for me"

Rebecca just shuts up and looks to Megan. Peninsky couldn't help, but to laugh in her face.

Megan: "okay, you two are going to have to chill with the foolish comments towards each other. Maronii, I am going to need you tonight for the Masquerade Ball meet me in the Ball room at 5."

Maronii: "that's not going to work; I am not going to the Ball"

Megan: "You are my Junior Journalist, you must be there that is Mandatory"

Maronii: "Well, that may be, but I talked to Ms. Lily and she has made me aware that sense this whole mess with Ms. Lexington's murder and I am a suspect that it would be best if I laid low for a while."

Megan's face was priceless; her nose became red and she huffed like a bull seeing red.

Megan: "well that isn't going to work for me."

Maronii: "It may not, but you're not the dean. Anyway why don't you have Rebecca cover you while you're there I know she would love it."

Rebecca: "Don't put me in this..."

Maronii: "You are already in this"

Megan was just pacing around, so I made my way to include the fact that Rebecca was playing 2 sides of the fence.

Maronii: "Rebecca is there a reason your even here right now?"

Megan: "She and I are working on our friendship. Why?"

Maronii: "Whatever lies you want to tell, I see through them. Don't you think after 4 years of school and you two not being friends that if there was a chance at that it would have happened before now, before I seen you talking to her in the town square, before she came by the library and dropped off those pages you ripped out of Ms. Jameson's journal, before she made me aware that you are just as crooked as she is?"

Megan: "What? Is this true Rebecca?"

Rebecca looked like she was relieved that I mentioned all of this. She turned around and looked at Megan.

Rebecca: "yes it is. I told you I would get you back you just never knew when or how. Now you want to call me your friend after you made a fool of me in front of the whole school. I am still facing that this very day. My problem isn't with Maronii, it's with you and now all of your true secrets are going to come out."

Megan: "you cannot do this. My history is not mine or yours to tell."

Rebecca: "Well that is too late; whatever Maronii is searching it will lead her to your family almost definitely."

Rebecca turned around and walked off

Megan: "Maronii, don't go searching"

Maronii: "You know my problem Megan is I thought that we were friends, true friends. But it seems that you don't even know what that means. As far as your family I have already been lead to their history it's no running from it now. I am just hurt that when I asked you about the Masquerade Ball you didn't mention you were in this. You just mentioned how if I was faced with lawsuits come find you, but this is something more. You could have easily told me that your family was a part of all the mystery around here. But you chose to keep it from me and lie and then run with Rebecca. The only thing is why you thought that you could trust her with Ms. Jameson's journal pages. That just goes to show me she is just as much a part of this as you are. I don't need your help so just stay out of my way."

Megan: "let me explain."

Maronii: "What?"

Megan: "My family is not the only family in this."

Maronii: "Tell me something that I don't know"

Megan: "Rebecca Chastens Grandmother used to be the dean here."

Maronii: "What?"

Megan: "Yes, here. In 1960 she was really good friends with my family, the Hawkins family and everyone else that was a part of the 1960 Class."

It hit me like a gust of wind. The picture of the Class of 1960... E. Chasten

Maronii: "What was her name?"

Megan: "Elizabeth Rebecca Chasten"

Maronii: "Well I have hit the jackpot on that one. Is that all Megan?"

Megan: "If you want to learn about Elizabeth Rebecca Chasten go to "Richland Nursing Home." It's about 30 minutes outside of town."

Maronii: "How do you know all of this?"

Megan: "Rebecca and I were friends before Hawkins, and like I said her and my family was close."

Maronii: "What about the Hawkins and Chastens?"

Megan: "Well after Penelope died, everything went haywire, the Chastens felt like they were owed considering they have been watching the school for years. But Penelope didn't see it that way she left strict instructions for the Hawkins School for Girls to be left in the supervision of a "Kind, dedicated, willing" Individual. Not the Chastens!"

Maronii: "So how did they take it?"

Megan: "How do you think? Next thing you know the Masquerade Ball was a new horror fest."

Maronii: "Okay, Megan I will call you later we got to go."

Megan: "Make sure you call me. And Maronii I know Ms. Lily didn't ban you from the Ball."

Maronii: "Okay."

Conversation ENDED!!!

I and Peninsky head over to the car, he was just shockingly quiet. I guess he could tell I was not in the mood, not after all of that.

Benny: "Is everything okay?

"Yes, we just need to get to this library"

Peninsky: "Maronii, how are we going to handle everything we just found out?"

"Peninsky like we have done with everything else, get to the truth. But we must see who DMP is and then we must go to the Police station to meet up with Detective Sully. We have 20 minutes!"

"Okay"

We head back into town, all the while I am still trying to open up this jewelry box. Then I notice the locket is in the shape of a key. DMP must have given this to Penelope as a set.

"Benny hand me the locket"

He hands me the locket, then out of nowhere...

"WATCH OUT!!!"

Out of nowhere we are hit by a car.

Everyone is so confused and shaken up; we look over at the other car and noticed it had a HG Cat on the window. Whoever it was they were from Hawkins Girl School.

We get out of the car, none of us was injured severely just a couple of scratches and a crazy headache for me and Benny.

"Benny, Peninsky this is Megan's car.... MEGAN, MEAGAN ARE YOU OKAY!"

Peninsky: "Maronii"

"What, what do you see?"

"This isn't Megan in here"

"What, this is her car I know it is. Who is it?"

Benny and I walk over to the Peninsky we take a look inside...

"Why is Lisa in Megan's car?"

Benny: "What the hell is going on?"

"I couldn't tell you Benny."

Peninsky: "Did anyone else notice that the car was coming towards us. Like it wanted to"

Benny: "Yeah I did notice that, that's why it landed on the side of us because I was turning over into the other lane while it was in our lane."

"Yeah, I saw that to."

Standing there figuring this out, school officials come out, the dean and Megan Parex with Rebecca Chasten.

Megan: "What the hell happened to my car? You did this?"

"I didn't do anything your car hit us, and on purpose at that Megan"

Benny was grabbing me in restraint and Megan was kept back by the security officers.

Benny: "Calm down Carmen its okay we are okay, my dad has car insurance"

"It has nothing at all to do with car insurance it is about we could have been really hurt and she comes out here talking about her beetle of a car. But Okay, I'm sorry"

He looks at me and kisses me gently and holds me. I am still shaken up. Peninsky was talking to the officers while the ambulance was getting Lisa out of Megan's car.

Dean Lily Sit Down:

Dean: "Megan Parex I need to have a word with you and Carmen Maronii"

We walk off to the side with Dean Lily.

Dean: "What the hell is going on Megan can you tell me why the hell there is a freshman in your car and why is she unconscious?"

Megan: Dean I didn't know she was in my car, I just finished talking to Maronii I had no clue."

Dean: "Hold that thought Megan. Maronii I have been looking for you and why have I been hearing that you are making a private case story out of the Stacy Dugal case?"

Maronii: "Dean I have been in my dorm for about 40 minutes I don't know why you couldn't find me. And as far as the Stacy Dugal case I haven't touched it."

Dean: "This is what you two are going to do and you're going to do it now. Megan you are going to answer whatever questions the police have for you and no one I mean no one is to write about this or talk to Lisa Fredrick's. Megan after that I need your help in the ball room. Maronii you go do whatever it is that you were going to do, but first get checked out by the Paramedics then later tonight I better see you at the Masquerade Ball no later than 8pm. If you have anything you want to discuss with me I will be at Medico Memorial with Lisa until she wakes up. I will see you ladies later. Get this under control and now."

SIT DOWN ENDED!!!!

The dean walks over to the paramedics and tells them she is riding to the hospital with Lisa.

"You put her up to it didn't you?"

Megan: "what are you talking about?"

"I know you tried to send her to my dorm room to get back Ms. Jameson's things so why wouldn't you talk her into trying to run me off the road."

Megan: "you have a crazy imagination Maronii. Lisa did this out of her own will; I guess I am not the only person you have angered on campus huh?"

"That may be, but she got the push from you and I will find out."

Megan just stared at me as I walked off. She knew that Lisa was not dead, so when she does wake everyone would know that she pushed this girl over the limit.

"Peninsky where is the jewelry box?"

"It's still in the truck."

"Okay, we're going to take my car. Benny, make sure your dad knows about all of this. You should stay until he gets here"

Benny: "No babe I am coming with you, the tow man has already said he will take it to my uncle's shop in town and I already called my dad. I am going with you."

"Okay, well let's go over to get my car and head into town."

[PHONE RINGS]

Phone Call:

DS: "Carmen I am waiting outside the station for you where are you?"

Carmen: "We are on our way we were in a car accident"

DS: "Do I need to send officers out there?"

Carmen: "No, your fine it's already taken care of. Give us 20 minutes and we'll be there."

DS: "Okay see you soon, drive safe"

PHONE CALL ENDED!!!!

We head over to my car and sped off to get to the station. Our pit stop at the library was going to have to wait.

Pulling up at the Police Station Detective Sully looked a little anxious and surprised to see us in such great condition.

Detective Sully Investigation Part-2:

DS: "What happened?"

“Well we were leaving to come into town, when one of my school mates drove into our lane and tried to run us off or whatever.”

DS: “What? Did they take her to jail, is she hurt?”

“Well she was unconscious and I suppose once they talk to her they will make a decision on if to press attempted murder charges against her.”

DS: “Okay, I am going to look into it.”

“Great, so now we are here what have you found?”

DS: “Well when you left I looked into Penelope Hawkins… Her maiden name was Penelope Chasten and she was not from Medico she was from Texas and last but not least it was claimed that she had a child or two down in Texas, but no one knows that for sure”

“What?”

DS: “Yep”

“I know that name and kids in Texas what the crap is going on?”

“Who is it?”

“The last name belongs to a girl I go to school with named Rebecca Chasten”

DS: “Okay well I will need to find this Rebecca Chasten and her family to find out if they knew of Penelope before she became a Hawkins”

“Don’t do that just yet. What else have you found detective?”

DS: “Well Penelope left behind a trust; I am still trying to get a hold of the firm who handled it. Of course some time has passed so it is probably not the same people, but the document should still be valid and kept somewhere down at city hall.”

“Okay, that’s great. Do you have any idea what the trust may say?”

DS: “Well it’s rumored that Penelope stated that “she was leaving the school to her first love DMP that she did not want any Chasten running the place and her kids were to be taken care of”

“Wow! DMP huh”

DS: “Yep that’s the rumor, but we don’t know how true that is”

I am pretty sure the part about who was supposed to run it was

DS: “Why do you think that Carmen?”

“Well only because Peninsky and I heard the same thing. Who told us I can’t tell you just yet, but what I can say is I would definitely look into the Parex family, Chasten Family and Fredrick’s as quickly as possible”

DS: “Okay, I will do that, I am going to need you guys to keep me posted on what you all find, so we can wrap this investigation up quickly as possible with as little damage as possible.”

“Okay, I have two questions Detective”

DS: “As usual Miss Carmen, shoot”

“Once is have you been able to talk to your superiors about getting Elaine Ferris to give the okay to Exhume Mrs. Hawkins body? And two is how do you know Jacob Peninsky Great-Great-Great Grandfather?”

DS: “Wow, you did have some questions okay. Well the answer to the first one yes, I have spoken to my bosses about Elaine Ferris they are taking their time with this one, I should hear something back this evening. The answer to your second question is Peninsky and my great grandfather worked together at the Hawkins Sugar Mill, before things went downhill for the family. You three might want to sit for this."

We all looked a little scared and Benny held my hand while Peninsky held my other hand.

When the Sugar Mill opened up it was like a ray of sunshine in a dark space. The Hawkins came with everything money, title and privilege then they started jobs and more. The town couldn't help, but to be loyal and respectful to them. I am pretty sure you all have already read the history books on the Hawkins family. Well that history book changes every decade depending on who is running the town and if there are any living relatives left. One thing it will never tell you is how this town went into chaos once the Hawkins provided jobs and money and all of their privileges.

The Sugar Mill was the prime bread winner for this town it supplied Sugar all over Alabama and other states as well. One day the Hawkins family met up to discuss dividing the profits from the sales throughout the family. With the divided profits there would be money that could go into fixing up the Mill. Well Charles Hawkins didn't see it that way. He wanted the Mill to stay put, he wanted it to show that being humble looks like that struggle, sacrifice, no privilege so he kept the Mill as it was.

Well around 1965 the Mill was ran down and just a mess, but the town kept it on just because it was a Hawkins contribution and the townspeople needed that Mill and by Penelope being gone and the kids gone Mr. Hawkins disappearance there was no will or trust or any living air that could say tear it down or fix it up. So the town left it, and the people continued to work there including my grandfather and yours. One day they were leaving from the mill and a roof pole fell and your grandfather pushed my grandfather out the way in the process he was struck by the pole. He saved my grandfather's life. Every year on my birthday my great-great-great grandfather would tell me and my brothers that story to remind us being here is never a right it is a privilege. So if Mr. Hawkins taught any man anything it was rights and privileges are earned either way try not to get them confused. I am sorry Jacob I didn't want to be the one to tell you that story sun."

We all just stared around for a while then Benny and I looked over to Peninsky.

Peninsky: "So you're telling me that my grandfather died for a privilege or whatever?"

Peninsky was upset and couldn't catch the reality of what just happened.

"Peninsky calm down, just breathe"

DS: "No I am not saying that; I am saying that your grandfather understood what Hawkins was saying, and he taught my grandfather something as well. Your grandfather died a hero and he was memorialized for years up until the Ferris boy's destroyed the monument we had it right over there a few years back. It was a sad day when that happened."

"What do you mean Detective?"

DS: "Well around 1995 there was this big falling out between the Chastens and those Ferris boys something about the Ferris boys through bottles at the Chastens home and work. Well the Chastens went around town destroying any memorial they could and your grandfathers happened to be one of those memorials. The Chastens were arrested, but let's face it in a small town privilege is important. The Chastens had money and power so they got out of that as well as the Ferris boy's they were Hawkins as well, so no one thought twice about sending them to jail. Pretty much after that I think both families felt they made a point so they just left each other alone."

Peninsky looked over at the circle in the square it is one way drive around all cars from different directions could come into the circle and go out other ends of the streets but dead in the center there is a fountain and some benches, really nice.

"Peninsky: so it was right there where that fountain is?"

DS: "Yeah, it was there probably 8 or 9 years before it was destroyed, but if you go over there you can still see the sign imprinted in the cement that says "Always Remembered Bravery and Dedication Lewis Peninsky".

"Peninsky: You really think it's still there?"

DS: "Yes, if not all of it some"

We run across the street and let Detective Sully show us the plaque

DS: "There it is, you can see a little of it, but you know it was there."

He pats Peninsky on the back and asks me can he speak to me alone.

"What is it Detective?"

DS: "Aside from this fatal blow to Peninsky how are you going to get Elaine Ferris to give permission to look at Penelope's body?"

"We're just going to go up there, you know what we will do that today. I have a question to ask you..."

DS: "Okay, well make sure you get her to sign these papers in order for this to be legal she has to sign. Now what did you need to ask me?"

"Well, you know Hawkins is having its annual Masquerade Ball tonight, I was wondering if you could get a few police officers over there to just keep an eye on things?"

DS: "Is there any particular reason why?"

"I just want us to feel safe. I wasn't going to go, but my Dean is making me"

DS: "Okay I will have a few officers come patrol and see what your suspicions are all about."

"Thanks, we're going to go ahead and get out of here head over to the library and to M.I.A then I will call you in a bit Detective"

DS: "Sounds like a plan Miss Carmen, YOU GUYS BE SAFE"

Detective Sully Investigation Part 2 ENDED!!!!

We say goodbye to Detective Sully and drive off. Peninsky was still a little upset, but not as much as he was before he seen the Plaque or before he knew his grandfather was a hero.

Peninsky: "So where are we headed now Carmen?"

"We are going to the library so we can figure out who the heck is DMP?"

Benny: "Are you okay Peninsky?"

Peninsky: "I'm great, just ready to wrap up this big mystery and bring back some honor to this messed up town."

Yeah, he was great alright he sounded like a feminine Vin Diesel that had imaginary steroids that weighed 130 pounds. We finally arrived at the library we parked and proceeded to head in.

"The first thing we do when we get in this library is to go back to the history section and find out who DMP is. Understood? After that we must leave so we can go to M.I.A"

Peninsky/Benny: "Got it!"

Walking over towards the history section we immediately started looking for section ML-H0290.

Benny: "I found it"

We rush over and began to flip open the book flipping through the pages, I noticed there was one already folded.

"Peninsky was this page folded down when you had the book earlier?"

"No, I didn't need to fold anything down, because the paper slipped out"

"Well someone recently folded this page right on Douglas Michael Parex. We found our DMP guys"

I looked around to see if anyone was looking and then I just ripped out the page and put the book back. We didn't have time to read page for page, it was already 3 o'clock we had a lot more to do

"Let's go guys..."

Elaine Ferris; Penelope Hawkins Exhumation Papers: Chapter 16 "I, Peninsky and Benny Hampton Investigating" Part 3

We got on the road and started our drive to 4400 Wellington's Lane also knows as Medico Insane Asylum.

"So this is the plan, we're going to go back in here talk to Elaine about getting Penelope's body Exhumed that's it, any other questions just hold them to yourself."

Peninsky: "that's fine and all, I just want to know what's on that paper you tore out the book in the library"

Benny: "yeah, me to."

We laughed, and then I opened up the torn paper.

"Well so far all I see is talk about how he was a copartner in the Sugar Mill and he had sons and a wife. Also rumored he had other children, but there was no proof of that. It says that his wife died of yellow fever she cursed Douglas when she died saying "she knew he had been with another woman and those rumors were true about him having bastard children."

Peninsky/Benny: "Is that all it says?"

"It has a little imprint; it looks like it says "Medico Print" why does that sound so familiar?"

Peninsky: "because that is also where the class of 1960 picture was generated or something."

"Okay, sounds like we have another place to visit once we leave Medico Insane Asylum"

Benny: "so, what are we going to ask Elaine?"

“Well, for starters we can ask her is it okay, if we see her today considering she sort of told us not to come back after our last visit?”

Benny: “Did she? Why didn’t you tell me?”

Peninsky: “yep she banned us. She bans us from seeing her. Who would have ever thought?” [Ha?]

Peninsky laughs to himself hysterically

“I didn’t tell you because if you remember you told us if we make her upset you were going to throw us out. Who would have known that you and I were going to be buddies?”

“Also Peninsky regardless if she should have or shouldn’t it happen”

Peninsky: “Okay, your right so what’s the plan after that?”

Benny: “well I think once she sees you with me she will ease up a bit”

“Benny is right we just have to play it safe and let her know we are not there to bring up anymore bad memories for her. Agreed?”

Peninsky/Benny: “Agreed!”

We pull up at Medico Insane Asylum and Peninsky and I look up at the building once more thinking we would never see this place again. Then I get a phone call...

Phone Call:

DS: “Carmen?”

Yes “Detective what’s wrong?”

DS: “The right channels approved the Exhumation of Penelope’s body”

“Great, we just pulled up at M.I.A”

DS: “Okay, well I will meet you at Hollows Ground Cemetery once you leave there do you have those papers that Elaine needs to sign in order for this to be legal?”

“Okay, that sounds great, and yes I do. Right here in hand, could you make a pit stop over at Medico Print before going to the Cemetery”

DS: “Yes, what am I looking for?”

“Ask them do they know anything about the class photo of 1960 and Douglas Michael Parex”

DS: “Okay sounds like a plan”

“See you in a bit detective”

PHONE CALL ENDS!!!

Benny: “What did Sully say?”

“That this is a definite go we just have to have Elaine sign these papers and we then meet him over at Hollows Ground Cemetery.”

Peninsky: “Hollows Ground, they say that place is cursed or something”

Benny: “I heard that to, but we must”

“You two stop your foolery and let’s just get this done”

We walk up the steps and once again I and Peninsky run out of breath.

Benny: "We should have just went through the employee entrance"

Peninsky: "What"

"Are you serious Benny?"

Benny: "What, it just hit me after walking up these stairs"

Peninsky: "I am going to save killing you for when I get my strength back"

Benny laughs and we walk into the lobby

Peninsky: "so how is this going to work Carmen, you remember what you said to Eugenist?"

I stopped with a certain urge to vomit; I forgot all about Eugenist, if she was here she was going to make it hell for me regardless if Benny is standing right beside me.

"Well let's just hope, she is off"

We walk in the first thing I do is look over at the front desk to see if Miss Eugenist is here. Looking over no one was here, not even the lady Judy. So my initial thought was to just make a run up the stairs and get Miss Elaine to sign the papers.

Benny: "So since no one is here right now we are just going to go ahead and go to see Elaine"

Seems like I was not the only one feeling the same way

Peninsky: "We could get in trouble"

Benny: "Peninsky, you could have gotten in trouble the first time, either way this is not unfamiliar to you. And we are not breaking in; we're just not waiting on personnel."

"Peninsky, just come on"

We head up the stairs, quietly and slowly, but quick enough where we could get to the fifth floor sooner than later. Stopping near the first red box on the second floor we hear a couple of orderlies coming down the hall, we quickly run over to a corner and squat to the floor. Peninsky was so nervous I swear he was sweating like a personal storm was over him.

Benny: "Okay there gone, let's go"

I felt like we were a part of "I Spy" or something, it felt cool and adventurous, but of course Peninsky felt differently.

Peninsky: "Couldn't we just came up the steps like normal visitors"

Benny: "We could have, but I am not at work today, and you're not allowed to be on the floor if you have no shift"

Peninsky: "Well can we hurry I can't stop sweating and I think I'm about to vomit"

'Peninsky you better grab a hold of yourself, we are almost there just calm down and keep focus."

Peninsky: "okay, okay!"

We come to the fifth floor, Benny tells us to wait while he checks the hall. Then he tells us to come on we run to Miss Elaine's room so fast I know I lost an eye lash.

Getting Miss Elaine to Sign the Exhumation Papers:

Benny: "Hello, Miss Elaine"

"Hello Mr. Hampton what are you doing here on a Saturday?"

We stood right behind Benny hoping he would smooth her over, before she had to see us.

Benny: "Well Miss Elaine I heard about the last visitors you had and I wanted to bring them to apologize"

"Benny, boy that's unnecessary"

Benny: "It just would make me feel better"

"Okay, if it will make you feel better I will see them"

Benny: "Thank you Miss Elaine"

Benny reached around to give us the okay. Miss Elaine was sitting in her window she had on a green dress with little sandals like she was going somewhere, she looked so beautiful considering the circumstances.

"Hello, Miss Elaine"

She turns around and smiles, as if she already knew we were there

Elaine: "Hello, Miss Carmen and Jacob"

"I didn't think you would remember us since our last visit didn't go so well"

Elaine: "Well Mr. Hampton here said you wanted to apologize so I thought I would give you a second chance"

"Thank you, we are really sorry we upset you last time; we were only trying to help."

Elaine: "I understand, but it wasn't that you upset me, it was the fact you thought coming to me would lead you to Stacy Dugal, without you doing the research to find out why she is dead in the first place."

All of us just stared back at her, like how did she know Stacy Dugal was dead?

"What do you mean Elaine?"

"Stacy Dugal is dead, and if she isn't yet she will be tonight."

"How do you know this?"

"Because I know of every descendant that has passed through Hawkins and the last are the Dugal's. Have you even looked into who they were or are?"

"No, I didn't think we needed to"

Elaine: "Well see there it is again, you're trying to figure something out, but you haven't started at the base dear"

"What is the base, Miss Elaine?"

Elaine: "The Dugal family do you even know how they died?"

"Well yes, they died at Hawkins?"

Elaine: "No, child"

"What do you mean?"

Elaine: "The Dugal's that died there were no older than teenagers, they weren't Stacy's parents"

"What?"

Elaine: "Stacy's parents were murdered the same way my husband was and I should have been"

"But, you said you tried to kill yourself and Robert, you found him like that"

Elaine: "That is true, but I didn't want to kill myself until I found Robert Dead."

"Hmm"

I started to think to myself about all these women in this family... Penelope- yellow fever, Douglas wife- yellow fever, Elaine- She attempted to kill herself, Robert- Killed Himself, Dugal- he killed himself and she killed herself.

"Miss Elaine if I wasn't in my right mind, all this would seem like a curse or something"

Elaine: "Well there you go Carmen"

Benny: "So you know there is a curse Miss Elaine?"

Elaine: "Of course I know there may be a curse, ever since the deaths started to happen and then my husband. I know I didn't kill him so who did."

"Well if this is true Elaine what curse is this, which is doing all these killings?"

Elaine: "What you have here Carmen is a secret that goes over 100 years ago, you find out about Penelope then everything will start to make since. But as far as who is killing that would be the one and only Charles Hawkins. I am assuming his remains were found?"

"How did you know that?"

Elaine: "Because we found the grave he was buried in when we all went to Hawkins. I, Michael Parex, Robert Ferris, and Lewis Peninsky Elizabeth Chasten, Hilary Norman and Beverly Jameson, Gina Lexington. We found him buried in Penelope's garden back in 1960. The same day we took that photo that I gave you on your last visit. I found a make shift plaque that had some flowers next to it."

"What did the plaque say?"

Elaine: "Lay forever in the love we had. PC"

"What did PC stand for?"

Elaine: "We were not sure who PC was and I still am not sure, but at the rate you're going you will."

"I have an important question Ms. Elaine?"

Elaine: "I figured you would. What is your question?"

"Why didn't you all report it?"

Elaine: "We did!"

"What?"

Elaine: "We reported it to, uh let me try to remember his name? "Myers something..."

Benny turned around and asked me...

Benny: "Myers, have you ever seen or heard of him before Carmen?"

"No, I haven't we have been working on this case for days and his name has never came up."

I started to think to myself, if this is the person who knew that Charles Hawkins was buried in the school yard. He should have come up somewhere.

"Miss Elaine who was this Myers"

Elaine: "He worked for Parex's dad. He did maintenance work at Hawkins and every now and then he would cut Parex's lawn."

I couldn't believe it. Myers worked with Penelope's lover. This was becoming even clearer.

"What do you mean Parex?"

Elaine: "Michael Parex's father Douglas Parex. He stayed at Hawkins it wasn't a day that he didn't stop by."

"Really"

Elaine: "Yeah, Charles and Douglas were best friends since Hawkins started the mill. Actually he and Charles started the Mill together he was on the board for it, but some years later there was a Meeting about the Sugar Mill being fixed up or something because it started to become run down a bit. So the board met up to divide shares and to discuss the fixing up of the Sugar Mill, but Charles Hawkins being the primary share holder he didn't want to fix up the Mill.

So the rumor goes, after that Douglas and he fell out and that was that. Penelope, Charles and Chastens, Parex's Jameson's, Lexington's were all good friends including Peninsky in the photo, but eventually things took a terrible turn after that. Charles begin spreading rumors that his children weren't his, that he was going to leave Penelope and all types of crazy stuff, but he never did and everyone knew he became a drunk and was always rambling.:

"Wow, sounds like Charles turned into a problem to some..."

Elaine: "you could say that, this town does have a lot of expectations of those who reside here. This town does crazy things to people. What haven't they done to stake a claim?"

"What do you mean?"

Elaine: "Well once Penelope died all the monies went to the school and some banked, but that was nothing. It was the hidden money of Charles Hawkins that everyone had sore eyes on. It was said that when he disappeared he took a boat to New Orleans, but before he left he buried the money in town where Penelope could never find it."

"Was any of that true?"

Elaine: "Well let's just say when they were looking for him, they were also searching for that hidden money. You can guess how that ended."

"Well. Could you do me one more favor Miss Elaine?"

Elaine: "Yes, of course"

"Could you sign these Exhumation papers for Penelope Hawkins?"

Elaine: "I was wondering when you were going to tell me about those papers"

I should have known she seen the papers

"I am sorry"

Elaine: "that's fine; I know why you're here. It doesn't bother me none, but like I told you on your last visit Carmen Maronii secrets are just a way of saying "stay out of my business". But if you want to go searching way in the deep I can't stop you. There you go!"

She signed the papers; we said our goodbyes and ran out of there quicker than we came in.

Heading to the car we saw Miss Eugenist. She hurried over to us to make us aware that she was reporting us for not being Elaine Ferris's family and that Benny could get fired. We didn't even respond we just drove off.

I told Benny to relax and look over all the notes I had taken and highlight some things while I drive and Peninsky as usual he fell asleep. It didn't matter he was tired and he had an overwhelming day so far. So we just let him sleep.

Benny:" Well it looks like we have another person to talk to"

"Yes, it does look that way Mr. Hampton"

We basically flirted with each other even though he was just a seat a way he made me feel like the girl who had won a million, billion, trillion dollars.

Benny: "So do you think that this Myers is still alive, or for that much still here in Medico?"

"Well that's what I was just thinking, if he knew of Charles Hawkins death and where he was buried he could have just left, but I am thinking he wasn't the only one a part of this secret so he might have just stayed."

Benny: "That is true. So where do we go from here?"

"Well we meet up with Detective Sully and give him these papers as well as mention this Myers person to him maybe he knows, he's been here all his life."

Benny: "Okay, let's do this"

We were just cruising when Peninsky popped up...

Peninsky: "Myers is not his first name"

Benny/I: "What?"

Peninsky: "Myers is not whoever this person is; it's not his first name"

"How do you know that Peninsky"

Peninsky: "Because he put the plaque for my Great-Great-Great Grandfather.

Huh?"

Peninsky: "When I looked at the plaque in the square it said Henry Myers"

Benny: "Is that who bought the plaque?"

Peninsky: "I am guessing he knew my grandfather well."

"Well now we have a name, so let's see what detective Sully comes up with."

I knew at some point of all of this I would find some secrets and some family drama, but I never imagined that I would get this deep into this whole towns past and secrets. I guess all will come to a head soon enough....

To be continued in Series Book: 3...

www.ingramcontent.com/pod-product-compliance
Ingram Content Group UK Ltd.
Pitfield, Milton Keynes, MK11 3LW, UK
UKHW041928190726
13854UKWH00004B/1506